I0738704

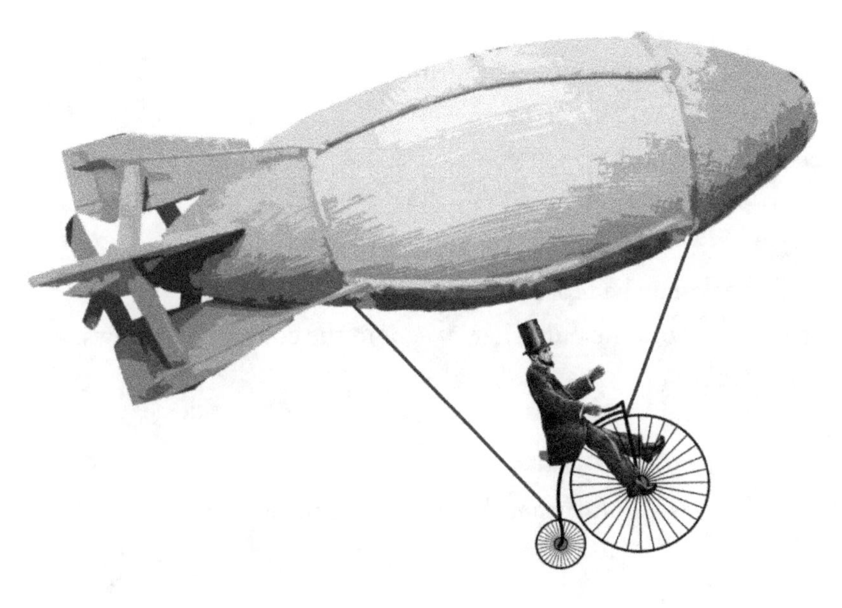

slantindicular

STORIES AMONG OTHER THINGS
A COLLECTION OF OBSERVATIONS

Katharine!

Published by
Sparkling Observationalist
sparklingobservationalist.com
thatkatharine.com

Miller, Katharine, 1979–
Slantindicular, stories among other things / Katharine Miller.

CONTENTS

MIRTH CANAL

EVERYBODY'S FREE (TO WATCH TV): ADVICE FROM THE TELEVISION SET

Ladies and Gentlemen, if I could offer you one thing, background noise would be it. The long term benefits of background noise have been proven in rec rooms and bedrooms for years, while the rest of my advice is nothing more than my own meandering experience.

I will dispense the background noise now.

Enjoy the power and beauty of classic sitcoms like *Dobie Gillis*.

Never mind, you will never understand the power and the beauty of Dobie and Maynard until they've faded. But trust me, in twenty years, you will look back and recall in a way you can't grasp now, how funny they were and how much impact Maynard G. Krebs had on the slacker generation.

Sing theme songs.

Don't waste your time with channel surfing. Sometimes there's something good, sometimes there's not. In the end, you go back to the first show you were watching.

Remember the good programs, forget the horrible ones. If you succeed in this, tell me how.

Stretch out on the sofa.

Don't feel guilty if you don't know what you want to do with your life.
Doogie Howser knew at 15 what he wanted to do. George from *Seinfeld*
still doesn't know.

Maybe Rhoda's sister will marry, maybe she won't. Maybe Martha Stewart will
do a children's show, maybe she won't. Maybe *Growing Pains* will have
a reunion show on their 15th anniversary and we'll remember Ben's real name.

Dance. Even if it's to a Rhino Records compilation CD commercial.

Read the small print on life insurance commercials, even if you have to squint.

Do not watch E!'s *Fashion Emergency*, it will only make you feel ugly.

Get to know your parents. They watch television, too.

Be nice to your siblings. They are your best link to your past and the people
most likely to join you around the kitchen table for a clip show.

Understand that *F*R*I*E*N*D*S* come and go, but there's always syndication.

Live in New York once, but leave before you upset the Soup Nazi.

Live in California once, but leave before you start saying "It's like, you know."

Accept certain inalienable truths, commercials will air, TV movies starring
Valerie Bertinelli will be made, U2 will get old and you'll fantasize that
commercials were witty, Valerie Bertinelli was a good actress,
and U2 was a great band.

Don't expect anyone to like the same shows as you. Use the remote for good.
Be careful not to lose it, but know that if it does get lost, it will turn
up somewhere.

Don't have the volume up too loud or when you're 40, you'll hear like you're 85.

Be careful which channels you watch, and be patient with the cable service
that provides it. Television programs are a form of nostalgia. Dispensing it
is a way of taking good ideas from the past, modernizing it and recycling it
for more than it's worth. But trust me on the background noise.

*written in 1999 as a parody of "Everybody's Free (to Wear Sunscreen)" and recently discovered
amongst the dusty bytes and pixels. We're having a .wav rave later. BYOBMPs.*

DON'T TOUCH THAT DIAL

My earliest memory is me at age three on a Saturday morning, alone in the living room, spinning around or whatever shenanigans a solo three-year-old can get into that would lead to breaking a lamp during the commercial break for *Laverne & Shirley in the Army*.

My second earliest memory is a short time later, watching our VHS recording of the CBS broadcast of *The Muppet Movie*, again alone in the living room, getting into whatever mischief that would lead to my lodging a pencil eraser in my left nostril during the Steve Martin scene. I waited until the end of the film before telling my mother because she specifically told me not to bother her with anything. And I figured I could still breathe out of the other nostril. I may have snuck into the kitchen to get pepper. Y'know, for sneezing. Because cartoons told me that was a thing.

I remember watching Teresa Brewer perform "Music, Music, Music" on *The Muppet Show* while my mother put the last of my father's belongings— his rattiest of underpants, his favourite kitchenware—in a box for him to pick up the next time he came to town. We were watching *Charles in Charge* when the moving truck took our furniture from the house we lived in to the small apartment where I would share a bedroom with my mother.

A lot of my memories feature television as a supporting character. My memories are cluttered with theme songs and commercial jingles, catchphrases and clip shows. I could tell you all about how televised content influenced me, inspired me, and impacted my development as a human being. Well, duh. Television was no mere household appliance—it was a member of our dysfunctional clan. It was almost always on. Get up in the morning and watch TV. Get home, have dinner while watching TV. Do homework while watching TV. Pull baby teeth while watching TV. Got the flu? Stay home and watch Phil Donahue.

I was always sent to another room to watch TV, usually because my family was watching something on our other TV. Television was not a treat. It wasn't a privilege to be snatched away. To deprive me of TV would've meant that my caretakers would have to deprive themselves—and actually watch me instead. Television was a staple in our media consumption diet, in a time before media consumption was a household concept. Our daily viewing surpassed the weekly average. If we weren't a Nielsen family, we should've been.

Television was my babysitter. Television was my teacher. Television was my best friend and constant companion. Television was my lifeline. Television taught me how to read, how to write, how to talk. It taught me how to live and love. It taught me about all the possible embarrassing scenarios one might encounter at dinner parties and big city offices. It taught me that if only I looked a certain way and used specific products, I could lead a glamorous, dramatic life. Television taught me how to be a detached observer of human behaviour.

You may imagine a small child sitting cross-legged on the floor, mouth agape, eyes wide staring up at a glowing set in a darkened room. This was not me. Ever the multitasker, I was colouring, building things, breaking lamps, turning my Little People hospital upside down and letting the Little People dolls carry on as if that was a completely normal orientation for a medical facility. Oftentimes, I would sit on my mother's bed with my back to the TV and enact stories with my stuffed animals. There was an ongoing love triangle between Kermit, Miss Piggy, and a large koala, with an was occasional disruption by slutty Rainbow Brite.

Television was freedom. In the era before parental controls, I was granted full command of the dial—such responsibility to bestow on someone still in their single digits. As cable was still in its childhood as well, my choices were often limited to what could be picked up by VHF and rabbit ears. Ted Turner and the Public Broadcasting Service provided enough compelling content to limit my exposure to static noise around the rest of the dial. My mornings would start in darkness, watching pre-1950s *Merrie Melodies/Looney Tunes* and Time-Life commercials for nostalgic album compilations—amassing my knowledge of Classic Hollywood actors and five-second snippets of the biggest Swing and Doo Wop hits. If *The Price Is Right* was on, it was time for lunch. If the soap operas were on, it was time for me to light somewhere and hush so the grown-ups could watch their stories. Sharing a room with my mother meant my lullabies were the themes to *The Love Boat* and *Murder, She Wrote.* Other kids had Saturday morning cartoons while I had *Monday Night Movie,* Sunday afternoon wilderness shows, Must See TV Thursday, TGIF, *Afterschool Special,* daytime game shows, very special episodes and the Weather Channel.

It didn't have to be good, it just had to be on.

My mother never told me what I could watch. I never asked permission. We would occasionally discuss things I'd seen and she would gently tell me which things were not really appropriate for little girls. Our chats about *The Patty Duke Show* would meander as my mother reminisced about going to a neighbour's to watch television as not everyone could afford their own TV sets yet. TV programs were black and white because the world was black and white, she'd tell me. The broadcast day was significantly shorter, there were three stations and half of them were fuzzy, and she lost both her husbands because she didn't have Donna Reed's domesticity or Annette Funicello's bosoms.

At my grandmother's apartment, I would hunker down near her 13" black and white set to watch *The Monkees* and *Gidget* as she whiled away the hours shelling peas and drinking PBR and talking about the impending end times. She, along with the visiting biddies in her Bible study group, loved to scold me for sitting too close to the television because it would ruin my eyes. They also scolded me for holding books too close to my face when I was reading. It never occurred to any of these people that my eyes were already ruined and the effect was not their theoretical cause.

For my ninth birthday, I was given a 4" portable TV/radio so that I could watch television anywhere, as long as I had eight C batteries and headphones. During school breaks, I would sit in my mother's office and watch *I Dream of Jeannie* and *Bewitched*. During tornado watches (or if I was feeling a bit lonely), I would bring my little TV and my potholder loom into our living/dining room and do my crafts while watching *Degrassi* or *Night Court* or *Amen* while my mother sat a few feet away and watched some hourlong dramas on the big TV.

With my prolonged exposure to screens, how odd it was to go to someone else's house and find that the television was not on. Children, if any were present, were sent outdoors. Women gathered and gabbed in the kitchen or maybe the fancy sitting room. In social circles where Bible studies were more prevalent than viewing parties, television was considered to be man's domain. Only when menfolk were present did the TV come alive, usually to blare some sports program or a western or maybe a rerun of *The A-Team*. I was not permitted outdoors with the dirt and the bugs, so I had to endure bitchy kitchen gossip or, more frequently, John Wayne whooping it up with Dallas Cowboys or something. Thankfully, I had a book. Okay, it was a *Charles in Charge* novelization I'd borrowed from my sister.

Time passed, life went on, networks stopped concluding their broadcast day with the national anthem and started filling the dead air with Time-Life infomercials. We all got slightly bigger television sets and expanded cable packages. Fifty-seven channels and nothing's on but we'll settle for the background noise because it's better than facing reality.

If I wanted to justify my family's dependence on television, I would reckon it was used as a deterrent, not only to discourage familial interaction but to dissuade outsiders from preying on an all-female household. Given our backwards state, is it really so far-fetched that someone could believe the blue glow of the television bouncing off our drawn curtains indicated a masculine presence? Maybe not if they could see we were watching *Falcon Crest*.

Televisions are everywhere now—sports bars, Chinese restaurants, coffee shops, shopping mall food courts, and highway rest areas. We're all staring

at screens for a significant portion of our day. We've got programs
on demand and a 24-hour news cycle to prevent us from spending too much
time with our own neuroses (while probably creating more). For all the choices
at my fingertips, I still turn to public television and Turner-based networks.

What will we do if we're suddenly and indefinitely cut off from electricity
and can no longer watch TV? Will we revert to the antiquated practice of
gathering round the family piano to sing the old standards? Do we know any
of the old standards? Do we even have any standards left? Will Time-Life sell
us the sheet music?

AN INTRODUCTION TO A GLAMPIRE

You Are Here. So says this mall directory. It's really "you are here"
scribbled on a neon orange sticker that's been stuck on this backlit map for
Eastdale Mall. And it is true, X marks the spot of this shady mall corridor with
the shoe repair, one of three nail salons, and a travel agent, which used to be
a comic shop or a collectable baseball card place. I don't need to be here.
I mean, I've been coming to this mall since before I could walk. I know where
all the stores are, that the flagship stores used to be Pizzitz's and Gaylord's
before they were Dillards and Sears. I just don't know why I'm here today.

I woke up this morning feeling a bit lost, so I instinctively came to the
mall, this shrine to commerce and capitalism full of shop windows glittering
with potential and promises—and price tags carefully tucked out of sight.
Mild dissatisfaction with life can be temporarily assuaged with plastic goods
and fried foods. I consider walking into the travel agency and asking for a one-
way ticket to Anywheresville.

I've been standing here, staring at this map, for probably fifteen minutes.
I'm lost in a daydream about some adventure where I become a new
Doctor Who companion and go off to do space battles. It starts where
I'm standing and the Doctor runs up to me and tells me he needs my help.

How's he to know whether I can help him or not? How's he get any of these girls? What if it's all some weird coma dream, like all these companion types are in comas and having these fantasies and the Doctor is just their real ordinary doctor filtering through into their dreamscapes? I never really make it to actual space battles because I'm always sidetracked by these questions. The fantasy and the reality of being approached by a strange man in a shopping mall are vastly different. In reality, if you're invited to join some random dude in his van, you're probably gonna wind up on tomorrow night's news. But I grew up with fanciful tales of girls running off and having adventures, sometimes stealing away with a mysterious gentleman, and I fully expected this to happen to me. Forget Prince Charming, I'd rather have the Goblin King or a Time Lord. Wandering these corridors of consumerism, I've often hoped a stranger would swoop in and offer the chance to go somewhere and do something, without care that it might lead to danger or death. My picture on a milk carton was the least of my concerns.

This is where I am when the voice behind me says, "It's weird how we never really get to see our own skulls, innit?"

The reflection in the mall directory reveals a man. My initial instinct is to remain still and ignore him in the hopes that he'll move on. Nothing good can come of an interaction that begins with a comment about human skulls. Right? He sounds British, though. Is he British? Is he the Doctor?

He speaks again, "I mean, there's x-rays and stuff, but that's all imaging. But it's like the one thing that belongs to us that no one's trying to tell us how to change or make it better because no one can see the thing. If we could, there'd be all sorts of bone whiteners and skull etchings and shit. Sorry. Shit. Have I freaked you out a bit? I've freaked you out. Shit. Sorry. I'm not a murderer. Of course, that's just what a murderer would say."

As he babbles on, I study his reflection. He looks pale but fit; his tight black t-shirt accentuating his broad shoulders and muscular arms, skinny red plaid pants, and silver Doc Martens. His hair black and shaggy. Atop his head is a tiny bowler hat fascinator. What is this dude's deal? Do I turn around? Do I run?

Apparently, I speak. "I'm Sarah."

Oh, I am going the right way for a kidnapping. My mom's gonna use that awful family photo from Christmas for the amber alert. Do they do amber alerts for adults? Might as well turn around and face the…holy hell, he's pretty.

"I'm Geoff. With a G…ah, and an O, I suppose."

Geoff with a G is wearing full eye makeup and shiny, bubble gum-tinted lip gloss, details not accurately reflected in the mall directory. He's pretty but not in a campy way. This is a man who knows how to accentuate his features. Oh God, I haven't eliminated all my embarrassing Instagram selfies. If this turns bad, the media will choose the one from my 26th birthday where sipping wine from an oversized bottle through a novelty straw while wearing an old-fashioned soda jerk paper hat.

He says, "You look like you could do with a bit of something. Adventure? Travel? A Cinnabon?"

"Which are you offering?"

"How would you like to join a ragtag collective of vampire pirates pissing about on a boat?"

An otherworldly creature offering a grand adventure? Fuck marriage and babies—this is every little girl's dream. Wait. "You're a vampire? It's 11:30 in the morning, though. And I can see your reflection."

"Yeah, there's a lot of misinformation spread about vampires. Like, we're not all sparkly bats who can be brought down by garlic and daytime. Brian does haves a garlic allergy but that just means we don't use pesto on pasta night…"

Geoff continues on about light sensitivity and different strains of vampirism. Do I go to mall security or dash off to the ladies room? He could be on the level or completely mad. He might actually follow me into the washroom.

"…while some doctors reckon it's a blood disorder that could be treated if we were willing to sacrifice our bodies for science. Bobby's put together a stellar pamphlet about vampire myths. He usually does the recruiting."

"Are you, what'd you say, on a recruiting mission?"

"Nah, I'm just here for a new pair of boots and some sunnies. But you were standing there, looking sad and lost and I thought you could do with some company."

It's a public place, I know all the exits, and I've got a penknife in my bag. What's the harm in taking a little stroll around the mall with this guy? "I could help you pick out some boots. Maybe you could tell me more about your... pirate boat?"

"Brill! Do they have bubble tea here?"

Geoff and I set off in search of boots and bubble tea. He notes that we're both wearing the same brand of dark blue nail polish, Midnight in Minnetonka. We chat about ironic t-shirts and whether Slim Jeggings is a brand of clothing or a crotchety old blues singer. Geoff says he likes to call himself a Glampire, which is fitting because he does love make-up and glitter and hair products. He's no Ziggy Stardust but more like if Bowie were a Girl Guides leader. His overall vibe is less *Labyrinth* and more *Troop Beverly Hills*.

Stopping to admire the mannequins in the Hot Topic window, Geoff declares, "It's really a brilliant time to exist. Everyone's a freak now. I love it!"

"So, how long have you been a vampire pirate? Vampirate?"

"Vampirate! Love it. You're a clever bird, you know? The guys are gonna dig that. How long have I been a vamper? Not very long, comparatively. I was hooking up with this bird after one night in a speakeasy, it gets a bit kinky and she starts biting me. It's like she's feeding off me and I go 'Wot's this, luv?' and she goes, 'Oh, I'm a vampire, I thought you knew.' Well, I just thought she was really into Victorian gothic shit. After that, I started feeling a bit sick and the doc gave me some pills, gave me a lecture about bloodlust and whatnot. And I been this fabulous thing ever since. That was, what, 1932, I think."

"Wow. And you were a pirate? Were there many pirates in the 1930s?"

"Well, we're not real pirates. I mean, we're not raping and pillaging and chasing after trunks of jewels. We're more like sea hobos; instead of stowing away on trains, we just hang out on this ship. We do steal things but rarely. We will torrent some movies and telly and we're always nicking someone else's wifi. Of course, nobody's volunteering their blood for nothing. But we try not to do murders. We don't like to rape because we've got too much respect for women. You might be surprised how many birds are actually into the idea of becoming a vampire, though. I think maybe we've got to stop dressing like rock stars when we go carousing. It might be the pleather pants.

Pleather makes women weak. Anyway, I was brought onto the ship in the '70s cos I happened to be hanging round the docks. I thought this bloke was looking for a good time, but it turned out he could sense I was like him, something about my aura or odor or, I dunno, Ambrose is an odd duck. He brought me to the ship, introduced me around and there's your fish. Am I going on too much? I always feel like I'm vomiting up my entire life story whenever I meet new people. I feel like I'm going on too much. Am I?"

"No, no. My thing is that I'm basically all questions and naturally, I'm curious about your whole situation and, well, there's just a lot to consider if I'm going to join you."

"Join me?"

"...Did you not ask...earlier? Oh, God. You didn't mean it. I'm an idiot."

"I did! I did ask. No. Yes. Of course, you're welcome! Come with us! Spend your gap year with us. Spend the rest of your life, if you like. We could do with a bit of fresh blood, sorry. New energy? Company is what we need. We're all bloody sick of ourselves and our stories are stale. We're shit pirates and we're shit vampires. It's a wonder we haven't driven stakes into our own hearts, really."

"Are you sure? Do I need to talk to Bobby? Sign a contract? Read a pamphlet?"

"Nah, I'm the cap'n. I can bring whoever I like and I like you. 'Course, I'm only captain cos we drew straws. Ambrose decided to retire to a castle, bit cliche if you ask me, and we had to pick a new leader. Teddy's got actual seniority, being the eldest. He even saw Billy Shakes live at the Globe! How wild is that? Clive and Owen are legit trained pirates from the olden days, so they handle all the boat stuff. Owen's got a wicked Powerpoint presentation teaching the how-tos of pillaging. Well, you'll see. Hm. I don't actually do any captain-y stuff. Maybe I'm more of a mascot. Are you hungry? Fancy a snack from the food court?"

In the words of The Clash—do I stay or do I go? Or are my new Converse hi-tops enough to ease today's discontent? If I don't go, I'll always wonder and regret the what-if. If I go, this dude might fashion my eyeballs into cufflinks. Or it will be a lovely time and I'll come back all the better for it. If I come back. It's a tired trope, the young girl dissatisfied with her life running away with enchanting strangers. Eventually she grows disenchanted and returns to normal life slightly wiser. It's not space battles with the Doctor. Well, I don't know what this is. Do I need to pack? I'm not impulsive enough to just pick up and take off! Do I need money? Sanitary products? Are there any ladies on the ship? Where will I sleep? I can't swim! Wait...vampires? Geoff is gonna have to answer a whole lot of questions over that Cinnabon.

"I don't think I've ever been properly introduced to anyone."

THE
ALGORITHM
REWARDS
NARCISSISM

AFTER THE TONE

The voices are getting to me.

They filter through me and each time I am forced to say the same thing to them. Over and over, every day, multiple times a day, it's "Hi, this is Bob. I'm not here right now, so leave a message at the beep."

I know secrets that no one else knows. I know where Bob's girlfriend was last night and why she called crying at 3 in the morning. I know how often Bob's coworker invites him over to "bond outside of the office." I know how much money Bob owes to debt collectors. I know that Bob's mom is worried about him and plans to visit soon.

I also know that Bob is here right now.

He's sitting on his couch, hand down his pants, watching television, and grazing on stale pizza. He's been there for three straight days.

Meanwhile, I have to listen to these voices. "Pick up, Bob. I know you're there." "Call me back." Fifteen different voices utter "Hey, it's me, pick up." Sometimes they just hang up. There's a cold, hollowness that comes from the click of the line after the beep. And I wonder, 'Why did you hang up? What didn't you want to say?'

No one ever calls for me. The message doesn't say "Hi, this is answering machine. I'm not here right now." I don't even have a name. But I'm here. They could at least say hello.

This tape is getting mighty full. Will Bob ever make the effort to cross the room and play back these recordings? Maybe flip the tape over to let his debtors record some B-side remixes of "Past Due" and "Final Notice." What if I just rewind myself and save him the trouble? I doubt Bob would miss much.

Ah, Bob rises! He's coming over, yes, here he is, pressing the play button. Get ready, you bastard.

"You have... 18... messages... Message One... (garbled voices)"

tape spews out of the machine

PEANUTS LOVE

You are my Charlie Brown
And I, your Peppermint Patty.
"You kinda like me don't ya, Chuck?"
I ask, you always reply, "Good Grief."

I am your Lucy, my heroic Schroeder.
As your number one fan,
I sit adoringly at the end of your piano.
I admire you, you reply "Good Grief."

In my heart, you are the fair Linus
To my Sally. I want to be
The blanket that you hold so close.
You are my sweet baboo, you scream "Good Grief!"

Oh, my Charlie Brown!
How I wish that I were
The little red-headed girl
That holds your heart, unknowingly.

THE OL' SHOP SKETCH

DISPATCH FROM THE LEDGE

I was supposed to change her life.

We first met three years ago, under the unflattering fluorescents of the neighbourhood Shoppers. She lingered in my aisle for what then seemed like eternity, studying every label of every product. It was late spring but her hair was mostly stuffed up into a lumpy toque, with two long strands attempting an escape behind her left ear. The toque was meant to disguise what she determined to be a bleaching mishap but could easily pass as an intentional style choice. That insecurity would be the cause of many late night drug store decisions. She stood directly in front of me, completely oblivious to my existence, as she considered the generic conditioners. She finally realized I was standing there all along and grabbed ahold of me as if she thought I was the answer to all of her problems.

She took me home that day and almost immediately took me in the shower. She was eager and determined and desperate, so sure that I would undo all the years of heartbreak and poor decisions—and almost immediately disappointed. I could only promise so much and it was clear I fell short of her expectations. Despite our failed first attempt, she kept me around. But she sought instant gratification while I demand commitment and patience, and what I thought would be a daily occurrence became an occasional dalliance. Eventually she started ignoring me altogether, leaving me to witness her continuing streak of bad decisions and terrible habits. She barely touched me. Now, to get called for duty is a religious holiday. I am drained slowly.

I often recall our first meeting. She hemmed, she hawed, the fluorescents hummed. Back and forth she went between the orchid and vanilla passionfruit and the island coconut verbena. How much time she spent comparing smells and costs and product descriptions! Did she want bounce and shine or lustrous radiance? Did she want to restore her roots or protect her DIY dye job? All that investment into choosing one of us and all of my benefits, squandered. She wanted a miracle; she needed me. We never really got started but, three years on, she can't seem to let me go. Lather. Rinse. Repeat.

When I took up residence in my spot on the ledge, I met my first mate. He was at half-life and intimated that he'd never had a companion in his time here. Our collaboration would be short-lived, but I estimated I wouldn't be too far behind him. Within weeks, he was gone while my shelf life continued to extend and my definition of eternity redefined. His replacement was a complete mismatch. We never had a chance of working together but were forced to stand shoulder to shoulder. Or shoulder to Head & Shoulders.

Occasionally a smaller, plucky sort takes residence next to me, his duty to protect the freshly coloured mane. He quickly finds we do not protect anything except the tub's ledge from muck beneath our bottoms. Lather. Rinse.

She could reach out to me so easily! If she would spare one minute. Sixty seconds more here and she'd save the three minutes she spends struggling against the tangles she's created. How much more smoothly her day would go if she'd just condition herself! Lather.

Living on the ledge, you see a lot of stuff. If you can call this living. I've been here for three years. I've seen colleagues come and go. Sometimes she brings in a perfect match for me but leaves me to watch him die a slow death. I once sat high upon a store shelf, surrounded by like-minded colleagues, all waiting to fulfill our duty. Now I stand with my back against the wall, surrounded by the residue of fallen comrades. The alchemy of moisture and dust have left a grey muck on my head and neck. It gathers around me. Mildew builds up behind me. The drain clogs before me. Lonely strings of hair stick to the tile above me. I was once part of a beautiful and fragile rainforest. I was supposed to unleash my herbal essences to tame and control and repair. Now she doesn't even pick me up to rinse me off. Rinse! Rinse, goddammit!

This is a room of great vulnerability as clothes and inhibitions are shed. It's behind the bathroom door where you'll find deepest insecurities unveiled and darkest confessions revealed. I've been audience to one-sided arguments and witty retorts come too late, performances of half-remembered pop songs and acceptance speeches, and utterances of wishes and prayers and regrets. I've heard the secrets that lovers keep from each other and the sobs of the lovelorn. From the tub's back ledge, we see all the worst angles. We are privy to the most delicate, what even humans have not dared to see—the backs of knees, the undersides of bottoms, and all those hard-to-reach places. We see the spots and lumps that go unnoticed for years but can change someone's life one innocent August afternoon.

I've looked on as she liberally applied shampoo to pixies and page boys, blunt cuts and bobs, and the unfortunate permanent, which, fortunately, wasn't. She's been brunette, blonde, ginger, black, and back to brunette again. Every change is an opportunity for us to reunite, to start that routine anew. Yet, here I stand, a bottle mostly full. Not that I'm alone in my neglect. I take solace from my view of a glass cabinet filled with lotions, creams, ointments, sprays, and capsules—a collection of whiteners and brighteners, all touting similar promises of life-changing results, some preceding my own arrival. The cabinet is a shrine to North American beauty standards of the new millennium. We look on as she pulls and pokes at herself instead of applying any of her products. She grimaces and grins at her reflection, inspecting every microscopic imperfection. She jabs her stubby fingernails into the red spots along her chin when a row of pimple creams and spot reducers are at arm's length. Her morning routine consists of toothpaste, soap, and shampoo. Is she saving us for some special occasion that never comes?

But, what would become of me otherwise? Had we stayed the course from the beginning, my end would've come along ago. And then what? My body is comprised of 20% post-consumer recyclables. Would I be refashioned into something more useful, more sustainable? Would I come back to her? Would I find new life in a landfill, giving more body and volume to seagulls' feathers? Would it matter? If the shower door slid the other way, I'd have been too busy to consider my own fate, just done and gone one day. Lather. Rinse. Repeat as needed.

Today, she looks quite different from our first meeting. Older, yes, but sullen and raw and bald. The toque fits loosely on her shorn scalp. She removes it and takes her usual position in front of the mirror. She doesn't poke at the red spots on her chin or pull at the skin around her eyes. She simply stares into her tired reflection. She exits and returns with a cardboard box, into which she deposits the contents from the glass cabinet. All of the bottles and tubes of emollients, exfoliants, salves, and balms tumble and clatter against each other as they land in the box. She turns her attention to the tub, picking out the dull razors, the body scrubbers, and the tiny remnants of forgotten soaps. She stops and stares at me, or perhaps through me, just for a moment and her gaze softens.

Now, after three years, I know her better than she knows herself. I know she'll never come back to me—at least not for the purpose found on my fading label, words penned by a copywriter thumbing through his thesaurus for another way to make hydroxypropyl methylcellulose sound sexy: Lather. Rinse. Repeat. I now realize that I bring her comfort. I am not merely a hair detangler, but a bottle of good intentions and the promise of a better hair day. A shinier outlook is just a dime-sized dollop away. I am her someday.

THE PLAN

Someone in this coffee shop is going to die. Well, he wants to die. Well, he thinks he wants to die. He feels like he's already dead, a ghost who has commandeered a human suit but has lost whatever it is that drives people to lead vibrant, productive lives. It is this feeling, or lack of feeling, that motivated Adam to pull one of the tabs on the "Considering suicide? We can help! Call this number" flyer on the coffee shop's community bulletin board. Unable to overcome his phone anxiety, he texts the number and receives an immediate reply to meet up this afternoon. He agrees and waits at his regular table.

The coffee shop is buzzing as the late afternoon crowd queues up for their post-lunch fix. It's always the same mix of business casual clientele bribing themselves with frothy treats to push through the rest of the work day, the bone-tired workers in danger of falling asleep again on their long commute home, and the telecommuters who ran out of coffee and clean pajamas at home. The other tables are full of the sort of characters you expect to see at three-thirty on a Wednesday afternoon. The gossiping high schoolers gab over caffeinated milkshakes near the window. Two business guys chug black coffee in their rolled up shirtsleeves while testing the boundaries of political incorrectness in banter and behaviour. Across the aisle, an ill-timed job interview is taking place. An employer's attempt to seem casual backfires as the overdressed applicant, already jittery from nerves, tries to overcome sweaty palms and dry mouth while sneaking sips of her latte between questions about what kind of animal she would be in an office emergency and what weaknesses will she have in five years. Adam's tiny two-top table tucked next to the condiment counter is prime observation real estate. He, however, is unaffected by the crowds, even as people lightly bump his seat as they load their coffee drinks with extra milk and sugar and the occasional dusting of cinnamon.

He takes no notice as Sue breezes into the shop and finds the quickest path to his table. Without hesitation, Sue seems to immediately recognize the man who called for help—the ratty college hoodie, the neglected neck stubble, the faint aroma of someone who said goodbye to good hygiene some time ago, vacant stare into the middle distance—Adam displays all the classic signs of a man who's not only given up hope, he's driven it out to a desert, chained it to a cactus, sliced open its belly and left it to bleed out alone in the sweltering heat. He barely blinks as she pulls the empty chair out just enough to squeeze into it and sets her oversized leather handbag on the floor.

"Adam?"

"Yes?"

"Hi, Adam, I'm Sue. I got your texts."

"Yes. Hi."

"So! You're planning a suicide!"

Sue's enthusiasm is just the thing to lift Adam's fog of indifference. He blinks and focuses on the young extrovert now perched across from him. Sue retrieves a business card from her bag and passes it off to Adam. The card reads:

Susan Smith

Personal Mortality Strategist

Adam studies her as she scrolls through her phone to adjust notification settings. Severe is the first word that jumps to mind—her hair pulled back just a touch too tight and her bun just a little too neat. She wears a navy blue suit, polyester with a fake light-blue pocket square peeking out from a fake breast pocket. The skirt length hasn't been in vogue since the early-aughts. The whole thing was probably bought in haste from a mall boutique for a job interview in the neighbouring corporate complex. She aims for successful entrepreneur look but falls just shy of a junior stewardess.

"Oh, erm, well...I have been thinking about it," he replies.

"Mm-hmm, well, as you know, suicide is a big step. It's a once-in-a-lifetime event for most people. I mean, it's a huge commitment. And it requires more preparation than you might think."

Adam nods and says, "I understand. I just don't know what my options are."

Sue reaches down to her handbag and pulls out an overstuffed binder which lands with such a thud as her sets it on the table that it even distracts the gabbing girls from their milkshakes and boy band debate.

"You called at the right time then. There are tons of options!" Sue opens the binder and starts flipping through pages of stationery samples, checklists, vision boards, and graphic scenes of suicide attempts.

"So, this is your first attempt at suicide, right?"

"Yeah."

"Good. We can start from scratch. What people don't grasp is that suicide requires a LOT of planning. Like, you have to decide how do you want to be found, what you want to wear, is it a destination suicide or an intimate home affair? How much are you looking to spend? Do you want to go cheap or spend every last dime? If you just wanna do something simple at home, that's a popular choice, but it lacks oomph. If you want to stage your event somewhere else, you have to book the venue, make sure you have the proper permits, and, oh, you've gotta hire a clean up crew! No one ever really thinks about clean up. And it doesn't matter how simple or elaborate, there's always a mess, but once the guest of honour is gone, who's left to pick up the pieces?

"Now, as a suicide strategist, I can source venues and provide all the paperwork, even make arrangements for any pre-event rituals or activities. Legally, however, I cannot be on site or assist at the time of the actual event.

"Have you given any thought to how you want to do it? Where? When? Like, a sunset suicide is really dramatic if you prefer to hang yourself, especially if you find the perfect tree on a hilltop. A silhouette corpse dangling from a tree against a brilliant orange sunset. Soooo stunning. Very *Gone With the Wind*. But you could also set it at your childhood home or outside the home or office of your biggest nemesis. Lots of options to consider."

Adam silently mulls the onslaught of suicidal possibilities laid out before him. 'Destination suicide? Who sets aside money to spend on killing themselves? Rich dying guys, probably. Is this what suicidal people think about, fantasizing over how they want to die? What if you haven't obsessed on your own dying moments, does that mean you're not serious in contemplating suicide?'

Sue turns her attention to her binder, flipping through her specially designed forms and worksheets for the client suicide checklist. She looks up from her binder and addresses Adam again, "So, have you decided on your method?"

"No. I mean, I guess I've considered a few things. I don't like pain."

"Who does, right?! Most of my clients inquire about painless and peaceful options."

"Like sleeping pills?"

"Surprisingly, sleeping pills are not that effective. There's a lot of romantic notions about overdosing when the truth is it takes a looooong time and it's not the pain-free escape that most people think. Overdosing is what you do when you're actually hoping to be rescued by your lover when they're about to break up with you or leave town. Actually, according to statistics, the most successful method in terms of lethality is the classic shotgun to the head. Go out with a bang is the surefire quickest method with the least agony, but it is messy and you've really got to have the motivation to follow through. If guns aren't your thing, there are other methods but the pain factor increases as well as the time it takes. You can really put on a show and set yourself on fire or literally take a flying leap, depending on how theatrical you want your final moments to be. However, your risk of survival does increase with those methods, so you'd need to be prepared for that likelihood."

In his 43 years, Adam had never thought about death and dying as much as in these last fifteen minutes. He wasn't sure that he really wanted to die.

'Isn't there some way to just...stop existing for a while? Has science invented invisibility yet? How can you disappear, guilt-free from responsibilities and expectations, but still be able to watch television?' As he considers the expense of suspended animation, Sue pushes on with her suicide checklist.

"Oh! Have you written a note?"

"No, I..."

"You really gotta leave a note. You don't want to leave your death open to speculation."

"I guess not?"

"Now, these days, people don't like reading so much, so you could make a suicide video for YouTube or even something super short, like a Vine or Instagram. You don't wanna leave a Facebook status update because that'll never show up in the newsfeed. Just between you and me, my business has nearly tripled since Facebook. I mean, jeez, no one clicked 'like' on the meme you posted four minutes ago and you think that's a reason to kill yourself? Like, c'mon! What's your online reach?"

"My what?"

"Friends, followers, subscribers...what are your numbers?"

"Uh, I've got a few followers on Twitter. My network is pretty big on Google Plus."

Sue groans.

"Is that bad?"

"I can see why you called for help. It'll be tough, but I think we can work with that. How far in advance do you want to organize this? Do you have a list of people to notify? Most of my clients plan about three months ahead, to give friends and family ample time to respond."

'Since when is death something to be celebrated and promoted? Are we really sending out invitations to our self-destruction? People arrange their own funerals,' Adam muses. He hasn't even told her that he wants to die. She hasn't asked. What would he say if she did ask? Does he even have a choice at this point? Adam decides it's time to speak up. "Okay, I phoned thinking someone would talk me through this."

"Yeah, that's what I'm doing."

"No, I mean, help me get past these thoughts."

"So, this is more like a cry for help thing?"

"Uh...I guess."

"Perfect."

"Perfect?"

"Yeah, you don't need a stranger talking you down. This is for close friends to rally around to give support. What better way to find who your true besties are than a suicide announcement?"

"Suicide announcement?"

"Sure, we'll print some invites and send 'em to your nearest dearest. We'll work out all the details for the event. Or you could throw a bequeathal, kind of like a bridal shower but instead of getting gifts, you'll give things away. Or we could go really simple with save the date cards."

"Shouldn't you at least try to talk me out of killing myself? Aren't you even going to ask me why?"

"Why? Why you want to kill yourself? Why does anyone decide to do anything? Why do people get married? Why do they get divorced six months later? Why do they throw lavish parties for puppies and newborn babies? Why do people hire specialists to clean out their messy closets? Why do people move across the country or across the world? Why do they volunteer in third world countries? Why do we cut our hair and get tattoos and go along with pretentious diet fads? We're all just grasping at something, anything to give our lives meaning. We need definition and purpose to our lives, otherwise what's the point? It's like we're all set on this path that we're supposed to follow in order to live the Ideal Life. If you stray from that path at any point, you feel like you've failed. If you discover the path is ultimately unfulfilling, you feel like a failure. If you decide to avoid the path altogether, everyone else makes you feel like a failure. Adam, do you have a job?"

"Yeah, but it makes me miserable."

"Do you think being a 'suicide strategist' is my dream job?"

"I really want to say no."

"Of course I don't want to be a suicide planner! I haven't had a steady, secure job since before the recession. I've got a master's degree in event management but there's only so many events to be managed by one company. I've tried doing other things—I've been a wedding organizer, personal brand consultant, bark mitzvah planner, personal grocery logistics and transportation coordinator, flash mob supervisor, and a personal priorities manager. Sometimes you fall down and sometimes there's no one around to pick you up and you have to decide whether it's worth picking yourself up and starting over again.

"So, why do you want to die, Adam? And why should I, a complete stranger, try to second guess your motivation? Who am I to say a life should continue or not? Do you really need someone to spew a bunch of life-affirming cliches while you're in your darkest hour?

"Did your parents stop talking to you? You've had too many failed relationships? You've been swiped left too many times or that job never turned into a career, and all your friends moved on with their lives and left no forwarding address? Maybe you've had to start over again so many times that you're exhausted and no one understands how hard it is to get up in the morning and send out another round of CVs and face another day of silent rejection. Maybe you've tried everything and have become so numb that you find no joy in anything. Sunrises and sunsets and raindrops and brownies and Julie frickin' Andrews herself just don't do it for you anymore. You've heard all the music, read all the books, seen all the movies and none of it sparked joy or inspired an interest in life beyond the dark void inside you?

"It doesn't matter what's pushed you over the edge to rock bottom or what put the last straw on the camel's back. The fact is you're here, so why not get some attention? So we send out announcements and write thank you notes to the few people who are still important to you. We go through every detail leading up to that fatal day to make it seem like the most important day of your life. Because it is."

The late afternoon rush turns to an early-evening hush. Aside from Adam and Sue, a trio of elderly Ukranian women discussing Canadian politics over tea have replaced the gaggle of teenage girls.

"Huh."

"What?"

"I never thought about all that. Death, life...living. I just shut down, became numb to everything. You've made some valid points. I failed or, rather, I feel like I've failed. I'm 43 with no family, no friends, no career. I was on the path and didn't realize early enough that I needed to take action to make things happen. I was always waiting for things to happen to me. And when things didn't happen to me, I just wondered what was wrong with me that I didn't get the girl or the job or the fruits of the middle-class American Dream placed in my entitled little hands without really trying. I was waiting for you to help me in the way that I've been conditioned to want help, all the while you have been helping me from the moment you sat down. I don't know how to fix my life. Can it be fixed? Can I take up a new hobby and find new passion without feeling judged that I left it too late? Do I want to? Is it too late to be discovered as an artistic genius or do I settle for being discovered some early morning, floating face down in the neighbour's above-ground pool? It's not your job to tell me what to do or try to fix me. It's not anyone else's job."

Adam reaches across the table for the binder, pulls it around to face him, and starts flipping through pages.

"You're sure this is the direction you want to go?"

"It's a jumping off point. I mean, it's something to do, at least. Most people aren't in control of their own death. Maybe some people buy burial plots and coffins, maybe people make a will, some create a mix tape to be played at their funeral. We tend to leave the actual dying up to fate. What if your death doesn't live up to your legacy? What if I can make my death more spectacular than my life?"

"Right. Okay. If you really want to start this process, here's my rate sheet. You'll see all the services itemized. Here, I'm giving a seminar on suicide planning at the Ramada Plaza this weekend. Why don't you come out, meet some of my other clients and get a better idea about services and whatnot?"

Adam turns to the invitation samples in the binder and pulls a simple cream-coloured card with a dark burgundy border from its matching envelope. "This looks nice for a bequeathal announcement."

"That is one of the more popular designs. I just attended one last weekend. It's a really good way to clear junk out of the garage!"

The coffee shop staff grows restless as closing time nears, becoming more intrusive with nearby tables and cleaning up the condiment station. Sue takes the cue and loads the binder into her handbag.

"Well, Adam, it was a pleasure to meet you and I think, going forward, we'll be successful in embarking on your end-of-life endeavour."

Adam rises from his seat for the first time since arriving two hours prior. He notices a slight ache in the left buttock of his human suit, likely from sitting on the round wooden cafe chair for so long. The twinge doesn't set off the usual 'all life is pain and why even bother' internal spiel. He grabs Sue's free hand with both of his hands and with all the sincerity his ghost pilot can muster, says, "Thank you, Sue. Really, thank you."

"No worries, Adam. We'll touch base soon."

Adam exits the coffee shop and starts off in the opposite direction of Sue. As he skims the back of the brochure for the suicide planning workshop, he notices how much lighter he feels. While not quite hopeful, he catches himself actually looking forward to the workshop and Sue. Beautiful, strange Sue. He's caught up in thoughts of Sue as he crosses the street that he is oblivious to the screech of the approaching truck.

Keep existing
BECAUSE QUESTIONING
MORTALITY
MAKES EVERYONE
UNCOMFORTABLE

TAN-IN-A-CAN

(a stream of consciousness exercise inspired by the lists of words found in rounds of Boggle)

Tan-in-a-can seemed a good idea at the time. The occasional orange-stained towel was a small price to pay for an exuberant epidermis. His honey-tinted limbs attracted honey-scented honeys to his side. And this natty cat couldn't say scat to these kittens. One hotsy-totsy played it coy and cool and lured the boy away from his harem. The kittens got catty, they hissed and they snarled as the golden goddess Diana reduced their Burnt Sienna Burt to a monosyllabic stupor.

He said, "Hey."

She said, "Nay."

As he started to leave, she said, "Stay."

He said, "Yay!"

Her glow was natural, his was a fake. Tan-in-a-can lead to love, loss, and lethargy. The occasional stained towel multiplied by hundreds. Now all he has left is a cyan cyst on his chest.

The climate change defier in his natural habitat.

OUT OF BODY, OUT OF MIND

I am now sitting in a small beige room. The room's only contents are me and this gray chair. In front of me is the only door to the room and a numeric keypad mounted on the wall beside it. There are no windows and no vents. The fluorescent overhead lighting fixture is mounted to a solid white ceiling. The flooring looks some kind of institutional linoleum. There are no mirrors or clocks or artwork, no magazines, pamphlets, instructions, or signs.

I don't know how I got here.

The last thing I remember is lying in a hospital bed, with the faint din and chatter of hospital staff and passers-by in the background and the louder blips and whirs of machines seemingly attached to my person.

I am not in a hospital gown now, just my regular clothes. I think these are my regular clothes. I've worn this sweater before but these shoes look different. Did I buy these shoes? They seem like shoes I would buy. I like them, anyway. This is the watch my mother gave me three birthdays ago. Is this the time? Hmm. The hands aren't moving. Either this watch has died or I have!

What is this room? Is this a waiting room? Am I waiting to be discharged from the hospital? Those must've been some really good drugs for me to not remember getting up and dressed and coming into this room. How long have

I been here? It feels like I have been waiting a while and no one has come in here to get me. Without a clock, I don't know if I've sitting here ten minutes or ten days. It can't be ten days because I've not gotten hungry or sleepy or the need for a toilet yet. When was the last time I ate something? I don't recall.

It feels very small for a waiting room, more like an elevator or a fully enclosed cubicle. Maybe it's an isolation booth. Why do I need to be isolated from everything except this chair?

Maybe I should just try the door. Why didn't I do that in the first place? Politeness, I guess? I don't want to push my way through if they sat me in here for a particular reason and I was still too drugged up to understand. I didn't understand most of why I was in the hospital anyway. However, this wait seems excessive, even by excessive medical wait time standards. Boy, I wish I could remember something. What if I was abducted from the hospital and brought here and certain danger lurks beyond that door? What lurks here but certain boredom?

I go to the door. It's locked. Is it locked or stuck? Locked. What if I turn the knob the other—nope. Maybe I'm too weak to open the door. I'll knock.

I'll knock louder.

What are the odds that I can guess the code for this keypad? Is it a three-digit code? Five? Four? I punch in all the obvious numerical password variations. Nope. I punch in every PIN code I've ever had. The handle doesn't budge.

Maybe this is one of those psych evaluation tests to see how long a person is willing to wait in a room or to what lengths someone will go to escape the room. I don't see any potential escape routes. If the ceiling were panelled, I could try to hoist myself up and see if that led anywhere. Or if there were air ducts, I could wriggle through those tunnels to…wherever air ducts go. Whoever designed this room certainly outsmarted me.

I try my birthdate on the keypad. The door unlocks. Finally.

On the other side of the door is a hospital room, different from the one I was in before. It smells of cigarettes and ammonia. My mother is asleep in the bed, with a newborn in a hospital crib next to her. She looks so young, so peaceful—my mother, that is. Babies naturally look young, except when they look like wrinkly old men. I move to take a closer look at this tiny, wrinkly old newborn—is this me? I examine the name band around the baby's ankle. She has my name. She looks like my baby pictures.

What...And how?

I stand here for—oh, look, a clock—twenty minutes attempting to process this experience. Maybe the drugs haven't worn off yet.

I don't want to disturb my mother, on any of the levels on which this would be disturbing. Maybe someone beyond her door has answers for me. I open the door to leave her room, to explore the rest of the hospital, but when I walk through the doorway, I am returned to my isolation booth.

Do I try to go back? Can I try punching in a different date? Do I know any other dates? My mother's birthday! Doesn't work. Dad's birthday! Nope. Lincoln's assassination! No...but I don't even know that I know when that was. Try some far off date in the future. No go. How about...my sixth birthday? Bingo!

I leave the beige room and enter my family's mauve and powder blue living room, where we're opening my birthday presents. No one acknowledges my entrance or notices as I walk around and sit on the piano bench next to Uncle Charles. I must be invisible. Time travel and invisibility? Why? Maybe this is a dream, one of those semi-conscious dreams where I can control some events but then the staircase turns into a dragon or something. Hey, this is the year I got my Dolly Pops and my Care Bear lunchbox! I wonder what my old bedroom would look like to me now. Still unobserved by the party revellers, I walk down the hallway to my childhood bedroom, turn the doorknob and... back to the tiny beige room.

So, I can travel through time, but only within my own timeline, where I am then invisible. If I try to pass through any door, it puts me back in this room. Isn't it time for some administrative sprite or anthropomorphic woodland creature to give me instructions or hints or a ridiculous riddle to solve to guide me to my purpose for being here?

I should try to find out how I got here. I punch in the day I went into the hospital. No good. Drat. I try every day before that to no avail until, at last, a day three months earlier. The door unlocks but I don't leave. What am I trying to do? If I'm invisible, how do I try to catch my own attention, to warn myself about...whatever this is? "Oh, hey, Self. I'm us from the Future and something happens where I can come and speak to you—what? Are we dead? Is this a joke? Is it a dream? I don't know either! Anyway, stay vigilant and take extra care around March 2015."

Even if I could proffer a warning, could I do anything to change the course of events that led me here? Or, is the thing that put me here a fixed point in my life, a kind of heat-seeking missile that will track me down and impact me, regardless of my lifestyle, dietary, or religious augmentations? The rules of time travel have never made sense to me.

Seriously, a guidebook or knowledgable elf would be very helpful right now. Where is that quirky guardian spirit whose ethereal career advancement depends on my escaping this magical isolation time travel booth?

If no one will answer my questions, I have to seek out the answers myself. Can I communicate with anyone? Can I touch things? Can I bring back mementos and liven up my little room here? Figuring that I have infinite time, and with no clues to the consequences of my actions, I start a series of experiments.

I go to my early childhood, back to my first bedroom. While my younger self sleeps, I search for clues and test the scope of my abilities with little impact on my timeline. I learn how to move things. While my toddler self plays with our stuffed animals, I confirm that I have no physical presence. No one can hear me speak. Or scream. I go to my friend Lindsay's thirteenth birthday party, where we played with her Ouija board in an effort to ask ghosts whether certain boys liked us. No matter how much ghostly ruckus I make, I cannot rouse myself or the other teenage girls. Lindsay stubbornly rejects my Ouija message that Kevin likes Kendra. If I can't prevent her heartbreak when Kevin takes Kendra to the Homecoming Dance three weeks later, what are the odds that I can keep myself from becoming an invisible time-traveling whatever-I-am?

I return to my old bedroom to practice moving furniture when I notice my father's copy of his Morse Code handbook on my nightstand. When I was 10 or 11, he tried teaching me the Morse alphabet and key phrases so that we could communicate with each other or I could signal for help. I wish he were here with me now. Does he have his own little beige room?

I try to shadow myself for long intervals. Sometimes I can follow myself for days at a time and I can accompany my Earthly self across the house, across town, across state lines. Eventually we walk through a door I don't recognize and I wind up back in my tiny empty room.

Maybe I'm not really travelling through time but just through my own memories. But what am I supposed to do? Do I revisit my own highlights? Do I relive the bad moments to discover what I thought were the worst experiences weren't so bad after all? I've been so preoccupied with looking for answers, I haven't really paid attention to the actual events I was popping into. Maybe I'm supposed to have a grand epiphany that will upgrade my dreary accommodations.

If these are my memories, maybe I'm not travelling at all. Maybe I'm in a coma and I lost those last three months of memories to trauma. What else have I lost? How long have I been here? Is it really so bad here? I am not in pain, I'm not cold or hungry or constipated or sleepy, I'm not even lonely. Do I really want to find a way back to paying bills and long lines at the grocery store and heartbreak and backaches and adult acne? Don't I want to go back to chocolate chip cookies and bacon and hot showers and cold beer and the smell of fresh laundry and stale farts and laughter and feeling?

My kingdom for a sensible cricket in spats and a top hat to sing a song right about now.

I go to the door and punch in my father's dying day. I know that's when I was sitting with him in hospice, holding his hand and telling him the banalities of that day's errands. I'm not sure why I choose this day, except it's one more desperate attempt to answer my questions before I resign myself to my little gray chair in my little beige room to sit, possibly forever. I watch my Earthly self tap Morse Code into our father's hand. I recognize it as a secret phrase he taught me. He tries to return the sentiment, but his hands are weak and slow.

Eventually my father drifts into a deeper sleep and my Earthly self nods off. This is the time to take a risk. I grab a spoon from his dinner tray and tap our secret phrase onto the wall. I hear it repeated over on the bedside table.

It doesn't seem to come from anyone visibly present in the room. I try it again. It repeats. This is the most excitement I've experienced in, well, who knows.

I tap frantically on the wall.

Dad? Yes! I have so many questions! Is this real? Where are you? I can't see you either!

I want to hug him! I want to speak! I tap and tell him all about my room and the time travel and the…what does this mean…if we're both here?

He taps back about his own room, which is the same as mine. He says he started by visiting all of his happiest memories—me, my mother, our holidays, Sunday dinners with his parents—and then looked for ways to move on. He tells me that he still hasn't figured anything out and that this is the first time he's had communication with anyone. He says he's been losing memories. This is only day he can access now.

We chat as best we can, for as long as we can. I tell him everything that's happened to me in the five years, minus three months, since he died. Soon, his body flatlines and the nurses flood in and in all the commotion, we lose each other again.

I return to my room. My cubicle. My isolation chamber.

I think about my happiest memories and which ones I'll revisit. The happiest moments never seem to be the big events, like graduations and weddings and birthdays. It's going for ice cream and stopping to watch a neighbourhood baseball game. It's a weekend nap with the cats snuggled up beside me. It's driving around at sunset on a cool July evening when your favourite song comes on the radio. But these are not moments you can type into a keypad and visit whenever you want.

In a fit of nostalgia, a craving for the hard rock of my youth to ease my current frustrations, I punch in a random day from my moody teenage days. The door doesn't budge. I try it again. I try the day before, the day after. I punch in my college graduation. No good. Have I already forgotten the date I graduated? I try my 21st birthday. The door still won't open. Am I already losing my memories? It doesn't feel like I've been here long enough.

I sit and I wait. It's really not so bad in here.

Suddenly, a buzzer. The door opens and a bright light floods in.

SLANTINDICULAR

As the conversation meanders from intellectual discourse about things
of which I know nothing to reminisces of shared experiences amongst the
parties in the room who are not me, so does my focus. I sit quietly on the
outskirts of the discussion group and, with little demand for my participation
or my attentive listening face, take a visual mosey around your living room.
The walls are lined with dated portraits of children and grandchildren frozen
in various points in time. These framed portraits are not on the wall, but
rather propped atop the chair rail, as if they were set there temporarily
and temporary came to mean 25 years. Everyone in the photos have aged
substantially in reality but there's scant evidence to that on display. It is here
where I first silently call your intent into question. Is this the result of
conscious choice, have you curated your wall decor by content or convenience?
Are these your proudest moments or are these merely the ones presented
to you already framed?

Other people's homes are cluttered with family portraits, obstinate
acknowledgments of achievements and milestones. The sitting room is a
shrine to ancient relatives, grandparents and great aunts and uncles dressed
in their Sunday finest commemorating anniversaries or perhaps a night out

to the Lawrence Welk show. The refrigerator is a collage of snapshots of life in motion—Polaroids from an aunt's party, Save the Date cards, picture postcards from a cousin's overseas trip. The living room shelves alternate Precious Moment knick-knacks with Kodak moment photographs. Kids in sports uniforms. Dad in his service uniform. Wedding photos. Graduation photos. The hallways lined with portraits from Sears or Olan Mills that feel like a retrospective on 20th century men's lapels. These are the families who send cards just because and attend every event and say "I love you" before hanging up the telephone.

My mother only kept a few professional photographs of her daughters on her bedroom walls, leaving the rest of the house free from familial faces. Perhaps you keep a corkboard in your bedroom pinned with the latest programs and snapshots, postcards and school pictures. What do the 21st century parents in a paperless world where all the photos are digital? Does Hammacher Schlemmer sell an Instagram frame that automatically streams loved ones' selfies and food pics?

The kitchen counter is covered with junk mail and loose stacks of paper. It is scientific fact that flat, raised surfaces naturally attract sundry paper goods. Every home has a drawer filled with dead batteries and dried-out ballpoint pens and a spot that collects magazines and expired coupons and catalogs and pre-approved credit card adverts. *The Ladies' Home Journal* tells us to sort this pile seasonally and to consider keeping a decorative basket on the counter to act as a junk mail catchall. Girls are conditioned from an early age to ready one's home for guests—for what if the Queen or the Pope were to make a surprise call to your home? Women's magazines tell us to tidy up and hide all the signs of everyday life. Don't subject guests to mysterious piles of papers or rogue socks or dirty dishes. The mismatched conglomeration of candles on the mantel can pass for decor while the assortment of aerosol air fresheners will not be viewed as a thought-provoking artistic statement on Man vs. the Environment. We do the tidying, not because we view our homes as spectacular showplaces worthy of a spread in *Architectural Digest* but because our guests have judgemental bones and waggling tongues. A single dust bunny tumbleweed drifting through the dining room could mean that Bridge Club is hosted at Agnes' house from now on.

The photos and the papers are par for the aged bachelor father course. Clearly you are not expecting tour buses full of royalty and architecture journalists to turn up on your doorstep. The rules of *The Ladies' Home Journal* do not apply to bachelors of an advanced age such as yourself. Bachelors of an advanced age are not expected to follow the rules of feng shui. Many bachelor pads are utilitarian, a sparsely decorated space where milk crates are shelves and lamps are placed according to need not style, the free wall calendar from the Audubon Society is strategically hung to cover a drafty hole, and the leaning tower of pizza boxes as the sole—and not wholly intentional—attempt at decor by half-sober frat boys. But what appears to be a mess here could actually be a complex system carefully devised over decades. You probably know why you saved the Travel section of *The New York Times* from January of 1996. You know the third envelope down the pile of random junk mail is a packet from AAA, which you intend to send back with a letter encouraging them to stop wasting so many resources on fake memberships cards and poorly organized pamphlets.

What has captured my attention and curiosity now is a seemingly innocuous word-of-the-day calendar on the side table, resting on top of a couple of telephone books from 2010. The word: *slantindicular*. Definition: *somewhat oblique; a portmanteau of slanting and perpendicular.* My chair is slantindicular to your sofabed. That picture frame is slantindicular to the floor. I wonder what the word was yesterday. Wait, today is not August 12, 2007. It has not been August 12, 2007 in nearly five years. Today is not even August 12 in any other year. What is your story, word-of-the-day calendar?

I have visited this house on two previous occasions, both taking place after August 12, 2007. On my first visit in October of 2007, it would hardly have seemed odd to see a calendar still set at August. Life happens! Who hasn't neglected to change their calendar at some point during the year?! It is possible that I would not have seen the calendar at all, in my blinding anxious panic to meet this intimidating patriarch who undoubtedly wondered about this fresh young tart who had common-law'd her way into your clan.

I was being introduced to the legendary father possessing a strong will and stronger opinions, high standards and higher expectations. I was keen to make a good impression, doing my best respectful nodding and putting on my attentive listening face and ignoring my surroundings. Or your surroundings. You were surprisingly convivial with me in spite of my remarkable stupidity and my disappointing deficiency in post-secondary education.

We've settled into our roles here and I am free to fixate on this calendar and its mysteries. Why does it stop on August 12? What happened—were you devastated because Merv Griffin died? Maybe you are fond of the word, having first encountered it in childhood. Maybe it sparked your lifetime love of words and now you chose to keep it on display. Maybe you hoped it would spark lively conversation about words and language, which were your livelihood for so many years.

It would be a very clever way to display your wifi password to guests, if you had wifi and guests.

Maybe someone gave you this word-a-day calendar for Christmas in 2006 on the premise that you liked words. Being of an advanced age, perhaps you determined that you knew quite enough words, thank you, but because the gifters were frequent visitors, you humoured them and faithfully tore off the pages once a day. Maybe they stopped visiting so much, and you only tore off the pages when you knew they were expected to pop by. Eventually they stopped coming around altogether and on August 12, 2007 you decided that was enough of that. The calendar drifted off into a corner of the kitchen counter, where other objects had also accumulated, and it simply blended in with the random assortment of crap.

It seems odd that a man whose whole life was dedicated to attention to detail would surround himself with uncontrolled chaos. If a stray comma could not escape your scrutinizing eye, how has this word-a-day calendar been set adrift amongst your possessions without purpose?

Perhaps this was the day you officially retired but there was no gold watch or commemorative plaque, just a sad word-of-the-day calendar to serve as symbol of the end of your career. In your home, maybe "slantindicular" came to define your retirement. If anyone asked how retirement was going for you, maybe you told them "It's slantindicular!" And people would think you meant "fantastic" or "great" or "just swell." I never thought to ask you about your retirement.

The likeliest explanation is that it doesn't mean anything at all and I am overthinking its significance and projecting meaning onto this minor ephemeral object. This is not your Rosebud. Although, who's to say there's no significance in the expired coupons that linger on the counter? Maybe they're souvenirs of a long-gone favoured pizzeria that was replaced with a Chipotle. Junk mail and old magazines and audio cassette tapes and forgotten correspondence and post-it notes with the password to a Netscape email account—none of it is irrelevant to a person's life, even if it is not of particular use at present.

I could have interrupted the nostalgic chat with my piqued curiosity. You might have waved a dismissive hand over it, said the nurse or the maid must've moved it or forgotten to throw it out. You might have offered it to me as a souvenir, maybe I could stand to learn a few new words.

The calendar is long gone now. As is the house. As are you. You have been scattered slantindicular to the wind. Whether any of it was significant to you, it is now significant to me. You and this word and this calendar are now inextricably linked in my mind. An unsolvable mystery. A reminder of the dangers of sitting quietly.

MYSTERY SOLVED

A distinguished gentleman, dressed for dinner but with a smoking jacket instead of formal dinner jacket, wielding a pipe addresses a room full of "suspects" for a mysterious revelation.

LORD ROLAND BUTTERFIELD-JONES OF HRMSFORTH:

I suppose you're wondering why I have gathered you here tonight. A great mystery has occurred here this evening and I'm determined to get to the bottom of it. I am speaking, of course, of how it happened that the keys to my automobile went missing.

As best as I can surmise, my keys disappeared between 4 o'clock this afternoon and sometime during dinner. You see, after dinner I was feeling quite agitated and supposed that a refreshing evening drive might alleviate some of my gastrointestinal distress. I went to the foyer to retrieve the keys to my roadster, only to see an empty key hook and my own dour reflection in the hall mirror. Who could've taken my keys? My car?! I dashed out to the garage at once to find my sporty coupe safely ensconced. A curious matter— Who would want my keys but not my vehicle?

As you are aware, preparations for Lady Agatha's bi-monthly formal gala—the one that clutters our main hall with the who's who of Whozzatshire—have caused quite a ruckus, with visitors swarming and flitting about and tradesmen traipsing through the house readying for tomorrow evening. Every caller entered through the main foyer and any one of them could have absconded with my key fob at any moment. But who had the motive? Which, if any, of these interlopers had incentive to commit Grand Theft Automobile Keys?

Let us review the goings-on of the day to suss out our key suspect—

The party planner met with Lady Agatha early this morning to finalize details for tomorrow's do. Then the decorator arrived to consult with Lady Agatha on wallpaper samples for the secret passages. Neither displayed any interest in motorcars.

I observed little Henry here, after breakfast, occupying himself with a set of jingling keys whilst plopped in the middle of the floor of the solarium. When I inquired after them, our butler, Thinman claimed ownership and responsibility as he'd lent his pantry keys to the tot in an effort to quiet him during one of Lady Agatha's headaches. Now, it's possible Henry toddled his way into the foyer, found himself mesmerized by my keys up on their hook, climbed the antique coat rack, and snatched them down. Hmm. Come to think of it, I saw Thinman nervously polishing my keys and returning them to the hook just after lunch. Odd little man.

Dear Lady Agatha retired upstairs some hours ago with another headache and hasn't been seen since. Even the arrival of her latest acquisition—a cricket diamond? The snooker sapphire? Badminton brooch? Baseball tiara? Apparently something that warrants throwing a party on Wednesday night —could not rouse her from her bedchamber. Her maid has been skittering up and down the stairs, fetching all manners of ointments and concoctions for her. I suppose she could have borrowed my keys at the behest of Lady Agatha, though for reasons I cannot fathom.

Sir Waggleston, the renowned kleptomaniac, has often been discovered transporting treasures to his underground lair in the garden. At the time in question, however, he was relentlessly hounding the nanny.

(bends to address dog in baby talk)

Weren't you, Sir Waggleston? Yes, you were. Yes, you were, my wittle snausage! Erf!

(clears throat, regains posture)

Where was I? Ah! right.

Now, the obvious suspect is my daughter Margaret, who came to me earlier in the day with a breathless desire to go driving, claiming it was a matter of life and death. Hmph, the death of my automobile most likely! I put the kibosh on that. She seemed anxious to get away—no doubt to see that lawyer chap who's been courting her with his vulgar Latin poetry, that Don Juan, Esquire. She was not at dinner, presumably still sulking as young girls will.

After that burst of drama, the locksmith came round to upgrade the locks on all the doors. Our last overnight guests complained about the large gaping keyholes into which wandering peepers could mosey. It seems unlikely that he would also replace the lock to my automobile, doesn't it?

Before I could escort him upstairs, the carpet man arrived to steam the Persians and air out the Orientals. He was followed closely by the party planner, who returned to inquire about the RSVPs from esteemed invitees. As I was about to direct him upstairs to Lady Agatha's room, he had the audacity to ask whether I would be fetching the prime minister from the aeroport before the event. Hmph. The PM can get his own ruddy ride from the aeroport for what we're paying him. He'll likely be boasting again about how he got his hands on the Duchess of Teacosy-upon-Noggin's newly augmented bust. He's storing the emerald-encrusted effigy at his flat next door until it can be presented at her birthday gala next week—thankfully not being hosted here!

Speaking of my dearest neighbour, Thinman announced the arrival of plumbers who were summoned to the cellar for emergency repair on the crumbling clay sewer pipes that lay betwixt our manors. The PM is forever moaning about the crumbling pipes of democracy backing up the flow of progress. The irony would be delightful if it weren't so inconvenient.

I was on my way to investigate the situation, when the carpet man and locksmith descended the stairs with a lumpy, rolled up rug that I recognized from Margaret's room. The rug man claimed Lady Agatha was sending it away for mending and so I sent them away.

As Thinman and I tried to steady ourselves from the whirling hubbub, an estate agent—bearing a remarkable resemblance to Margaret—wandered in unannounced. She just happens to be selling a comparable property down the lane and asked for a tour of ours. I led the charming agent through the rooms as we chatted about tomorrow's event and all of today's commotion, housing prices—it's astounding what properties sell for these days! Maybe I can convince Lady Agatha to downsize if she ever tires of throwing these lavish parties. Nora, the agent was absolutely enamored of my old coupe out in the garage and insisted that I take her for a ride one day. Imagine that!

Well, with all this activity, it's no wonder dinner turned my stomach into a dance hall!

After discovering that my keys had vanished, suddenly, the electricity went out! I heard three screams, including my own, followed by an eerie silence. I groped around for a torch and, upon finding one, made my way into the library. While turning to sit in my favourite armchair, I felt a sharp pain in my lower rib cage and fell to the floor. It was then I discovered that the key to my automobile had been in the left pocket of my waistcoat this entire time! Ha! Can you believe it? Oh, of all the things. Wait 'til I tell Aggie about this.

He puffs on pipe and wanders away.

Same Time, Next Year

slantindicular

October 29

THE HEIST

(a stream of consciousness exercise inspired by the lists of words found in rounds of Boggle)

Two tots plot to stop a heist at the pier. The first tot spots the men planning to shift tin. Tot two spies the men's hens, shapely ladies man the getaway van, waiting for the heist to begin. As the men hit their mark, the ships dock. Faceless drones unload the hot lot of pots. With a wiggle of their hips and jiggle of their tops, the ladies entrance the drones with their womanly wiles. Our men swiftly snatch up the lot and scurry to the getaway van. As the drones begin to get fresh with the flesh the men employed for distraction, the tots emerge from their pits and land a few hits on the spit.

The cop with the tip from the tots of the heist of hot pots arrives on the scene just in time. The hens run to the men and the cop follows the flesh-baring fiends. As the men start to give the slip to the hens and the close behind cop, the tots set a trap for a trip. They tie a rope 'tween two posts and pin the men to the ground. The hens quickly confess to their role in the mess and the cop handles the rest. After foiling the heist at the pier, the two tots have a fest with soda and pie. The end.

*"I should've read the Terms and Conditions
at birth more carefully."*

CMYK

Born into Avocado and Harvest Gold
Pristine porcelain from red mud
Pretty in pink in spite of the blues
A world struggling to remain black and white
While "Shades of Gray" plays on the radio
Pastel mornings over pastoral mounds dull by comparison
To dreams of neon electric nighttime
Intermittent turquoise and magenta illuminate discotheques and corner shops

Roy G Biv and Bell Biv Devoe
The spectrum, the prism, Benetton's United
"Raspberry Beret" and Apricot Freeze
Atomic Tangerine and the Shamrock Shakes
Taste the rainbow, nothing tastes like orange

Early promotion from bubblegum to rogue
Virgin's Blush by day, Whore's Kiss by night
Nude control top and long-lasting lipstick irony
Party like it's nineteen ninety-beige
The girl in the grey flannel short skirt and long jacket
Black tights and white cats in the concrete jungle
Monochromatic modern so fresh, so feh so fast

Sun-faded cyan ghosts haunt the discotheque posters in corner shop windows
How soon then it comes for lime green pantsuits and blue rinses
The porcelain cracks

Survived by silver holographic jumpsuits and platinum hairdos
Fade to black on stainless steel

INCESTRY DOT COM

On a wraparound porch of a family farmhouse in rural Alabama on a sweltering early August evening, two white women sit in rocking chairs and sip iced tea from mason jars. The older woman has a folded paper towel wrapped around her mason jar glass.

MAMA: 60+ woman
BABY MAE: 45 year old woman

MAMA: Lawdy, but it's hot!

BABY MAE: Yes'm.

MAMA: I don't reckon it's been this hot in a mighty long while.

BABY MAE: Weatherman Ron said it's gon' stay hot for the foreseeable.

MAMA: You'd think it'd cool off once the sun sets, but it jus' don't do that way anymore.

BABY MAE: Lots of things ain't like they used to be.

MAMA: Go tell that, Baby Mae!

BABY MAE: Hey, Mama.

MAMA: Yea'huh?

BABY MAE: I'm fixin' to be 45 in a little bit.

MAMA: Mmhmm.

BABY MAE: D'ya think we could change my given name from "Baby Mae"?

MAMA: But you are still my little Baby Mae.

BABY MAE: It's jus' real hard to be taken seriously at work. Cain't I just be Mae?

MAMA: Then how we gon' tell you apart from Mammy Mae?

BABY MAE: Well, Mammy Mae's up in heaven and I'm here.

MAMA: We still gots to pray for ya both. Besides, you done okay for yourself up to now. And "Judge Baby Mae Williams" sounds real good in that courtroom. Your cousins been real proud to have you presidin' over their bail hearin's and whatnot.

BABY MAE: It's come to my attention that most of them boys ain't real cousins.

MAMA: We all god's children and we all related in some way.

BABY MAE: Even the monkeys?

MAMA: Only Cousin Michael.

They rock in their chairs and fan themselves.

BABY MAE: Lawdy, it's hot!

MAMA: I cain't think straight.

BABY MAE: Maybe if we don't think about it, it'll be more tolerable.

MAMA: Alright. Well, why don't you tell me what's been goin' on with you baby girl?

BABY MAE: Oh, nothin' much. I tried goin' online to look up our ancestry for granny's birthday, 'cause I heard you can do a search and find out iffen you're related to famous people and thought she'd get a kick out of learnin' we're connected to Robert E. Lee or Paula Deen or somethin', but I ain't find much on us yet.

MAMA: Well, we ain't much for bein' online, since your brother got in trouble with the law for lookin' at all them pictures of nekkid girls.

BABY MAE: It don't really work that way, Mama. I put granddaddy's name into the ancestry site but there was too many Willie Johnsons. And a surprisin' number of them had daddies named Ezekiel Johnson. I don't suppose you got more specific details I could use, like where was they all born and who came over from the U.K. and such?

MAMA: (*sighs*) You know, you a real bright girl, Baby Mae. I don't know how you ain't figure this stuff out all on your own yet.

BABY MAE: What stuff?

MAMA: Your daddy ain't your real daddy, for one.

BABY MAE: He sure done behaved like he ain't my daddy.

Wait, who is my real daddy then?

MAMA: Your uncle.

BABY MAE: Your brother?!

MAMA: No. Your daddy's brother.

BABY MAE: My uncle's brother?

MAMA: Your uncle's brother is really your uncle. And his brother is really your daddy.

BABY MAE: That's not confusin' at all! But granddaddy is still my granddaddy?

MAMA: Yes'm. That is...if your granny's telling the truth. She got around with a buncha fellers in her day. But you got to understand that was a different time, Baby Mae. A girl could court several boys 'till one of 'em had to marry 'er.

BABY MAE sips on tea and mulls over this new information.

BABY MAE: Mama?

MAMA: Yeah.

BABY MAE: You mean to tell me you were with my daddy and my uncle-daddy?

MAMA: Well...no.

BABY MAE: So, my sisters are my sisters or my cousins?

MAMA: They are your sisters in the ways that count.

BABY MAE: Mama, are you really my mama?

MAMA: I'm as real a mama as you need.

BABY MAE: ...You're not givin' me real satisfyin' answers here.

MAMA: Well, you know your big sister?

BABY MAE: Margie or Girleen?

MAMA: Margie.

BABY MAE: I believe we've made acquaintance.

MAMA: Well, she had a dalliance with your uncle-daddy one time and didn't tell nobody 'til you come out.

BABY MAE:So...my sister is my mother and my uncle is my daddy? And you're really my grandmother?

MAMA: If you want to look at it biologically, then, yes.

BABY MAE: This is one mangled family tree.

MAMA: I don't think we got but the one branch.

They sit quietly, continuing to sip tea and fan themselves.

BABY MAE: Gotdang it's hot!

MAMA: Watch your mouth! You ain't too big for a s witch.

BABY MAE: Mama? (*scoffs*) Mama.

MAMA: Yes, Baby Mae.

BABY MAE: I jus' don't know how to deal with all this.

MAMA: Most of us take to the drink or the bible. Sometimes both. A hollered-out bible makes a good hidey-hole for a flask.

BABY MAE: Bless y'all's hearts.

MAMA: Lawdy, it's hot! Baby, go fix us some more sweet tea.

BABY MAE: Yes'm.

Baby Mae exits and everyone needs a shower thinking about how these white people think they are the superior human beings.

THE BACKSEAT GOES WHERE THE FRONT SEAT GOES

It's 11:30 on a Friday night in the summer of 1989. Most young people are out with their permed mullets and jean jackets having Swayze-fueled times of their lives. I am in the backseat of my mother's car, with my mother sitting beside me, the front seat populated with my 21-year-old sister and her 23-year-old lunkhead boyfriend. We're on the first of many family road trips to Florida. We will make this exact same annual trip over the next five years, getting lost five more times. In the summer of 1991, when the lunkhead in the driver's seat is my sister's husband, I will be eager to point out how many times we've gotten lost in this exact same way. My mother, again seated beside me, will grimace knowingly and remind me that no one likes a know-it-all child.

Here in 1989, rings and vows have not been exchanged, and yet my mother is allowing this young boy to drive her car. This car that isn't quite paid off and that no one is allowed to eat or drink or fart in and whose insurance policy probably doesn't cover this stubborn Southern good ol' boy with a passion for spectator sports and music performed by men in cowboy hats and just happens to be dating her eldest daughter. The white Buick Century has dark burgundy velour interior and little chrome ashtray compartments in all the doors and the seat back. I like to play with the compartments, flipping the lids and thinking up other uses for them. I am not allowed to put gum or empty gum wrappers or coins or secret notes in these ashtrays. I am not really allowed to put my fingers into the ashtrays. But I do it anyway. There are four of these ashtrays in the back seat. My mother is not a smoker, but I suppose car manufacturers were not producing non-smoking cars in the 1980s.

In winter, I am not allowed to draw shapes or letters on the fogged up windows with my greasy child-sized fingers.

But this strange boy with no sense of direction and a low threshold for distraction can drive this car. No one can even offer to take a driving shift when we go off track. My mother, with her phobias of highways and poor night vision, cannot trade places with the boy. My sister has yet to get her driving license and can only control the radio and the air conditioning, neither of which ever offer relief to the backseat.

The boy is a smoker, but he is not permitted to smoke in my mother's car. He is, however, allowed to use his dipping tobacco. He expels the "dip-spit" into a 20-ounce bottle that used to contain Mountain Dew. This bottle will be full by evening's end.

Despite the number of dip-spit vessels that will accumulate in her home in the future, dipping is somehow a more acceptable habit to my sister. In the years following this trip, the couple will argue over his smoking. My sister will outright forbid it in her house. Early on, the boy will accept the challenge to quit smoking along with the additional challenge of lifting weights in his afternoons after work. "Working out" comes to mean watching Ricki Lake (and sometimes pornography) and lifting the occasional beer can. He sneaks the occasional cigarette, but he's bad at hiding the evidence. When his dream of having a six-pack means drinking it all before dinner, he negotiates with his wife that he will stop smoking if he can grow a beard. She finds beards to be significantly less attractive than the prospect of a fit hubby but reluctantly agrees. He grows a beard and sneaks cigarettes.

This will go on for too many years.

I cannot have a strawberry milkshake or french fries in this car. He can have an unopened bottle full of brown tobacco-tinged spittle tucked between his legs in the driver's seat.

It is always 11:30 that we find ourselves tired, grumpy, and carsick scanning the road with bleary eyes for cheap—but not sleazy—vacant motels. Given the option, the boy would just pull into a rest area and nap until sunrise. His girlfriend is in that delusional phase where she thinks the boy believes that she wakes up with hair done and a full face of fresh makeup, a phase will continue well into their marriage. She will not sleep in the car. My mother would stuff the boy in her trunk if she didn't fear the legal ramifications. I probably dozed off for an hour or so.

It's a four-hour drive to our destination, theoretically. We're to meet up with his family and stay in their beachfront timeshare for the weekend. We leave after work and try to take a side highway to avoid rush hour on the interstate. The boy thinks he knows the route because his family traveled this way all the time when he was a kid. But he doesn't really know because normal kids don't pay attention to things like exit numbers and on-ramps. By the summer of 1993, I will know the exit numbers and recognize all the tiny town names and all the landmarks, like the abandoned convenience store with the fading old-fashioned Coca-Cola sign and that one boiled peanut stand and the other boiled peanut stand and that tree that looks like Sweetums from *The Muppets*. My mother will remind me that no one likes a smart-ass teenager.

On this trip, I have brought a couple of Anastasia books by Lois Lowry, two notebooks, and my small collection of cassette tapes to play in my white portable boombox. When it gets too dark to read or write my secret story about the ginger boy from my class who also lives in our apartment complex, I sit in the dark and think about my ginger boy while pretending that this Phil Collins song is about us.

The boy brings his radar detector in case he gets the chance to speed along these two-lane county roads. Along the rural back roads of lower Alabama, the detector blips rapidly, frequently. The boy talks of speed traps and cops with their quotas. Do policemen actually have quotas for tickets issued in any given period? Is this a myth perpetuated by bitter male drivers who feel unjustly targeted? The average American Redneck is apparently born with lead feet and an over-productive speed gland.

No one thinks to make travel plans at a time when perhaps policemen aren't eager to make their ticket quota.

The AAA map might as well be written in Sanskrit as none of the car's four passengers can really make sense of the squiggly lines. Well, my mother can but refuses to interject this time. My sister will be mortified if our mother challenges the boy in any way. We are supposed to be a normal family, going on a vacation with his normal family and we are going to make normal family memories if it kills us.

There's road work and lanes blocked around Troy, which slows traffic to a snail's jog. The boy tunes in a football game on the radio, so he can alternate between yelling at the log truck in front of us and whatever displeases him about the game commentary. The boy always wants to listen to the game, despite the fact that the game always upsets him. My sister would rather listen to cowboy rock or Air Supply, but she's letting him have his way because she wants him to believe that she is a Nice Person. However, she is desperate to get in on the yelling action, but instead of upsetting her boyfriend, she directs her anger at me and the Rock of the '80s compilation cassette I'm enjoying. The faint sound of Kenny Loggins' "I'm Alright", it seems, can be heard through the tinny headphones over the radio, road noise and redneck rage. She sweetly demands that I turn it down. She's jealous because I have my tiny bit of freedom in my boombox while the boy listens to the game.

My mother is quietly white-knuckled in the back seat with me, no doubt mulling what lie to tell in case of an accident. Will she have to somehow swap places with the boy to climb into the driver's seat if there's an accident or if the radar detector is faulty and we get pulled over? Will she claims he's her son and it's okay for him to drive her car? Will she play the dithery old woman who doesn't know the rules? We can't afford a ticket or an accident or even an extra night at a motel that we're stuck with because it's too late to do anything else.

The boy gets lost after stopping for gas in Opp. We're halfway to Andalusia before my mother sneaks a look at the map and tries to gently hint that we've gone off track. The boy curses under his breath. My sister says we'll just turn around at the next exit. My mother will not suggest that there's another road that we can turn onto to get back in a southward direction because the boy insists on going the way his family drove for years and it really shouldn't take this long. There is nowhere to turn around for another 30 miles. My sister is panicked. My mother is anxious. The boy is probably frustrated and embarrassed. I am sleepy and bored because it's dark and woodsy and that ginger boy is never going to think of me in a way that will inspire him to write Casey Kasem to play that Phil Collins song as a long distance dedication to me. In her panic, my sister turns around and hisses at me to turn off my goddamned music or else. Because absolute silence is a surefire cure for being lost on a rural road near midnight. At least we finally made it across the state line.

By 1994, still no one has the foresight to book reservations at a place that's a reasonable distance between the highway and a gas station. Everyone still expects we'll make it to our intended destination in one night. At 11:30, we're still approximately an hour and a half from our destination, theoretically. And we will still spend half an hour driving around a slightly bigger town in hopes of finding a cheap motel with a front office that's open late nights and doesn't terrify my mother. The only differences are the car is paid off and I can have a Coca-Cola in the backseat.

Eventually, we are freed from our motorized prison and drag our crumpled selves into a slightly bigger space to pass the time 'til daybreak.

These are our traditions. This is what we call vacation.

This is us having fun.

SNOWMANO A SNOWMANO

slantindicular

Ack! You've disfigured me! But how?!
Dude, I'm just standing here!
Look at the thermometer over there. It says the temperature is just above freezing.
Aha! You've activated a secret device that raises the temperature just enough to wipe out our entire race! Putting your evil doctor science to work, I see.
Why? Why would I do that? If I destroy you, I destroy myself. I destroy my wife and children...
Oh! How are Lucinda and the boys?
Cindy's got a great job at the ice hotel. We just got a new igloo in suburban Siberia. The boys are perfect little snowflakes, as always. What about you? You still with, er, Evelyn?

slantindicular

Doesn't this all seem a bit silly? I mean, I've got a scary face, you've got superhero hair, but aren't we really just the same? We've got to share this lawn for, I mean, who knows how long we'll be here... maybe a week, maybe a month. It's us against nature. Don't you think we should strive to get along while we're here? Enjoy the moment, the company, the view!
I know that I have sworn to protect this lawn from evil. Whenever there's a snowball fight, I'll be there to guard the fort. Whenever a teenager tries to steal the lawn jockey, I'll be there. Whenever a rogue dog tries to pee on this tree, I'll be there. For as long as there is snow on the ground, I am Major Fluffy!
Right. Great. well, I'm not planning to steal or pee on anything.
I know... because I've got your Melt Ray. Take that, Pineconeface!
DOC-TOR PINECONEFACE!

BITTERSWEET SIXTEEN

I do not want a Sweet Sixteen party.

I am supposed to want a Sweet Sixteen party.

I am supposed to want to wear a pretty dress and invite my best gal pals over for presents and cake and do whatever it is girls in pretty dresses do at parties. Melissa, my older sister has offered to host my Sweet Sixteen party, despite my objections. Our history tells me that she what she really wants to do is put on a show that I call "Love's Baby Soft presents *Every Girl's Dream Sweet 16 Party as Seen in a Magazine Advert or Perhaps a Popular Television Show About Teenagers.*"

Melissa is ten years my senior, but she sees herself as perpetually sixteen. Melissa is now a homeowner and wife and mother-to-be, which should make her behave more like a grown up, but the more life experience she gains, the more immature she becomes. She may be downright infantile by the time she becomes a grandmother. She's always eager to talk about the cute high school football players, but only about their physical attractiveness and what it might be like to kiss them and not about how the quarterback recites the Pledge of Allegiance using only armpit farts. Yes, sister dear, that put me off idea of kissing the quarterback, too.

We are constantly feuding over the Right Way of doing things.
I am strongly opposed to the Right Way—or the traditional "this is the way
it has always been done and therefore should always be done forever and
ever, amen" way of doing things. Simply because people have been doing
things a certain way for a very long time, does not mean it is good or right
or appropriate. Our family life was nontraditional in a time and place where
following tradition had a great impact on your social standing. Melissa bore
the brunt of our broken home and lower-class life in a middle-class town.
She craved conformity and normalcy and looked forward to doing things
the way they've always been done and assimilating into white-bread
suburbia. Nontraditional is the norm and many of my peers also have tired,
single moms and don't care what gets between them and Calvin Klein jeans.

My sister turned sixteen during our mother's separation and divorce
from my father. We were broke and in a new town far away from her
friends. Her social network consisted solely of fellow teens who'd been
coerced into attending Jehovah's Witness meetings with their parents, too.
There was no way she was getting a Sweet Sixteen party like her old friends
were having. Now she has the means and opportunity to throw a nice party.
Too bad her kid sister is such an impossible jerk about it all.

The party is doomed from the start. A Sweet Sixteen party is supposed
to be something akin to a debutante ball for middle-class girls, a coming out,
an announcement to the gentlemen of society that this girl will be a woman
soon. It's the celebration of an arbitrary age chosen by men of a certain age,
with the perception that growths had spurted, figures had filled out,
and consent could be given freely, with minimal grumbles from rolling-pin-
wielding mamas.

Hello, boys!

Our mother, the pacifist is staying out of the fête fracas. She is not
concerned about rites of passage and comings of age or celebrations
of any kind, but she is too tired to fight Melissa. Instead, Mumsie sighs
whenever I complain about the party. "Just give her what she wants,
Christine," she says. "She's just trying to give you a nice party. It'll be over
before you know it. And she's already bought the decorations for her kitchen."

Melissa's house has been transformed into a "Barbie Throws a Birthday Party for Skipper" playset. It is a "Sweet 16" party-in-a-box, with pink banners, pink plates, pink candles, and pink sheet cake. It's more saccharine than sweet. This is not a party put together for me, but a party held in my honour. Like when someone makes a donation in your name instead of buying you a gift, it's a good deed, done with the best intentions, but do you really get anything out of it?

This party is being thrown for a 16-year-old girl that Melissa imagines is her sister—the little girl who likes wearing pretty dresses and make-up and enjoys shopping and talking about boys and daytime television dramas and loves all things cute and feminine. I really hope this girl shows up and gives us all a break.

We were never going to be debutantes, but this is underwhelming for what was supposed to be the marking of an important milestone. Even by "nice party" standards, it's Lamesville. Why, this is the apex of my life. This is the age that pop songs and movies and television and serialized young adult novels have romanticized for decades. Since the invention of the teenager, crooners have extolled the virtues of the sixteen-year-old girl. These are the halcyon days when your knees don't hurt and you don't have to balance a bank book. Sixteen is the perfect age, when you have a modicum of freedom—you are capable of independent thought and opinion but you don't yet have any of the responsibilities that come with living in the modern material world. Maybe you have a car, maybe you have a little job. You are thin, you are supple, you have hair in all the places where society expects you to have hair without mocking you for it. You have a lifetime of opportunity stretched out in front of you. I have accepted that teen life is not a John Hughes movie. It is not Saved By the Fast Times of Parker Lewis 90210. The realities of sixteen are far from the fantasies of sixteen, where 25-year-olds play 16-year-olds.

My friends are a rag-tag mixture of genders and classes and races. Thanks to early onset puberty, a couple of the kids could easily pass for 25. Mostly, we're a bunch of lumpy, bespectacled, spotty, gawky teenagers who will fall out of each other's social orbit in two or three months time.

If Melissa had wanted to lead an underdog sports team to unlikely victory in a sporting event championship, she certainly put together the right bunch.

My guest list is small and subject to host approval, which means I will be surrounded by people my sister has met and approved, regardless of whether they and I are more than casually acquainted. She is disappointed that this boy-girl party will not include any of the popular, attractive people she's seen around our football games. She is not impressed that we've got the *crème de la crème* of the high school newspaper and the award-winning marching band.

I don't have a boyfriend. I had a boyfriend during the previous school year and then there were boys I was "talking to" but not "hanging out with." One of three boys I've been "talking to" this summer gets invited because his mom is work friends with my mom. We chat on the phone in 15-minute increments, but it's mostly my saying weird things and his responding with monosyllabic grunts. I'm not convinced he likes me, much less "like-likes" me, but he keeps calling and Mumsie won't let me change my telephone number. So, here we sit in awkward silence on Melissa's dusty rose sofa. I keep a safe, platonic distance from all the boys in attendance because I do not need my sister to attach romantic significance to them, even though she has vocalized her distaste for them because they are not cute.

Instead of an inseparable group of girlfriends, I am surrounded by School Friends (we are comfortable enough to crack jokes within the school walls, but never make extracurricular plans), newly-acquired acquaintances, and future enemies (they know who they are), most of whom do not know each other. Everyone is polite but conversations are stilted because most of us are barely on speaking terms. I dropped one too many truth bombs with my on-again, off-again best friend recently and we are currently off-again. She's here out of spite, although I'm secretly glad she came. When we are on-again, we will laugh about this terrible party. My best guy pal brings his girlfriend, to the chagrin of Mumsie, who had hoped guy pal was boyfriend material for me because she thought he was cute. One of my new friends brings her younger brother, who turns out to be well-versed in Monty Python, providing me with some rare moments of levity in what feels like an eternity but is actually only two hours.

No one is leaving this house with new friends and a broadened worldview.

I hid Melissa's compilation CD of party music I think was titled "Now That's What the Hit Parade Thinks Teenagers Like and Definitely Not an Excuse to Sell Soda-Pop and Deodorant", so she's retaliated by making us all sit in her living room without ambient music-like sounds of any kind. Mumsie offers to sing The Crests' "Sixteen Candles" except that she only knows the first bit, so it becomes a medley of all the oldies songs that she can remember that mention "sixteen" somewhere in the lyrics and she trails off with the chorus of "Que Sera, Sera."

After 45 minutes of awkward greetings and the swishing and clinking of ice cubes as we sip our pink Sprite-based punch, Melissa switches from passive chaperone to bubbly social director.

"Let's do the cake!"

"Okay, everyone squeeze in for pictures! Smile, y'all!"

"Now let's open presents! Ooh, what's that? Who's it from? Oh, that's so sweet! Where'd you get that? Aww, I want one of those! Say 'Thank You,' Christine."

She falls back on clunky conversation starters, like,

"How do you know Christine?" and —

"What do you study in school?" and —

"What's your favourite scene in Grease?" and —

"Do you know Jason the Quarterback?"

I'm ready to go home and start the process of turning the day into a distant memory, never to be revisited. Mumsie tells me that it's rude for the guest of honour to be the first to leave. She also tells me not to do anything to upset my sister. So I endure Melissa's last-ditch attempt to liven the party, when she says, "Why don't we go around the room and say something about Christine?"

What could have been a series of pleasant speeches, toasts, or roasts turns into a quick mumble of "She's nice. Yeah, and funny. I don't really know her well, but I hope we keep in touch. Uh, she got good grades in that class we were in together, so she's smart? She did a thing one time that was okay." Real yearbook quality stuff, guys.

After the very brief extemporaneous comments, I suggest a round
of Spin the Bottle to pass the time. Everyone laughs. And then we sit quietly
for the last 20 minutes of the party, with only the sounds of masticating sheet
cake filling the air. What I wouldn't give for an armpit fart sonata right now.

It's my party and I'll be in the bathroom crying if anyone needs me.

FAILING THE BECHDEL TEST

Two sisters hanging out in their shared bedroom while the youngest girl, SYLVIA gets ready for a date.

SYLVIA: age 15, baby of the family, relaxed and fun-loving.
ANGIE: age 18, second youngest in the family, grounded and studious.

ANGIE is lying across her bed reading a college textbook. SYLVIA enters in a robe with a bath towel over her head.

SYLVIA: Angie, I can't find my favourite purple shirt. Have you seen it?
ANGIE: It's in the closet—
(SYLVIA opens the closet door and removes towel from her head, tossing it onto ANGIE'S bed)
on the floor—
(Sylvia crouches down)
under your dirty clogs, two pairs of pants, four magazines, and what I can only guess is your towel, still a little damp from yesterday's shower.

SYLVIA rises and pouts as she picks up the towel from the bed.

SYLVIA: Oh, well. Thanks for letting me use your towel. Rufus spilled shampoo all over the tub and used the other towels to try to clean it up. The giant bottle of conditioner remains untouched.

SYLVIA puts the towel back on her head and dries her hair.

ANGIE: No problem. I guess I'll do the laundry tonight while you're out on your date.
SYLVIA: Snore. Why don't you go out with your friends?
ANGIE: They all have dates tonight.
SYLVIA: Well, don't just do chores around here, Cinderella. Watch some TV, put on a dumb romcom or something.

Angie scoffs and returns to her book. Sylvia drapes the towel across a chair and grabs a brush from the nightstand. She brushes her hair as she paces around the room. Angie sets her book aside.

ANGIE: Nervous about tonight?
SYLVIA: Maybe? I think I'm more excited than nervous.
ANGIE: What's the guy like?
SYLVIA: I don't know much about him personally. He's a friend of Molly's brother and they set us up. I've met him a few times, but we've never hung out together on purpose. He's polite, though, a nice guy, reasonably attractive.
ANGIE: *(mock swoons)* Why, he sounds good enough to marry!
SYLVIA: Oh, hush.

Sylvia looks at her clock.

SYLVIA: I should finish getting ready. He'll be here in a few minutes and I wanna meet him outside.

*SYLVIA grabs a dress from a pile of clothes on the floor and changes behind
a dressing screen.*

ANGIE: You aren't bringing him in to meet the family?

SYLVIA: And let our brothers go several rounds with him? I barely know
the boy. I'll bring in a guy I know I don't like to sacrifice to the savages.

ANGIE: The Pitter boys do get a little crazy when it comes to protecting their
little sisters. Why do you think I don't bring people around here anymore?
Anyway, I need to get a look at this...what's his name?

SYLVIA: Charlie.

ANGIE: I need to get a look at this Charlie so I can see what passes for
reasonably attractive nowadays.

SYLVIA: C'mon Ange, you've dated cute guys before. Cute is still cute. You
know it when you see it.

ANGIE: Maybe, but my boy-watching opportunities are limited these days.
And boy-meeting is even more rare.

*Sylvia emerges fully dressed, except for shoes. She grabs her hairbrush and perches
on the edge of her bed to brush her hair.*

SYLVIA: What happened to all the college guys you were gonna date?

ANGIE: Enh, I'm just not the type of girl they're after, I guess.

SYLVIA: Pfft. They're dumb then. Hey, what about that boy from your
Intro to Ergonomics class—Stanley? He had quite a thing for you.

ANGIE: He is not *my* type.

SYLVIA: Aw. What's wrong with him?

ANGIE: Well, I like to think I'm open-minded about people and their quirks
and peccadilloes, and I hope it doesn't seem like I have impossible
expectations for guys I want to date, but I do prefer that my boyfriends
to know how to tie shoelaces. I think sometime between puberty and high
school graduation, you gotta give up the Velcro sneakers.

SYLVIA: He wears Velcro shoes? Dude, that's dorky. They're just shoes, though, right? You could probably ask him to wear loafers or something.

ANGIE: It's not just that he wears them. When we're sitting in class, he likes to sit behind me, put his feet up on the back of my chair and pull on the Velcro strips. Noisily. Slowly. Repeatedly. *(imitates the sound of Velcro peeling)* I don't know if he's trying to get a rise out of me or if he just likes the way the peeling Velcro sounds echoing through the auditorium. But I can't talk to him anymore without hearing the sound of crackling Velcro.

SYLVIA: Weirdo. Maybe I'll ask him out.

ANGIE: Don't you dare! ...He might make a good sacrifice, though. *(sighs)* Oh well. There will be other boys for other days. Tonight is all about you and Charlie. Are you going to the movies?

SYLVIA: Maybe. Charlie just got his license and an old car, so he may be more interested in cruising around than sitting in some crowded movie theatre.

ANGIE: Hey—no parking. Small towns and backseats are the primary reasons why our older brother and two of our cousins are getting married this year.

SYLVIA: It's just an innocent date. I don't even know if I want to hold this boy's hand. I just like to look at him is all.

ANGIE: Just be sure that's all you do.

SYLVIA: Yeah, yeah.

ANGIE: I know. But it's better that you hear it from me instead Charlie hearing it from our brothers' fists.

SYLVIA: Yeah. Hey, what did Mom tell you before your first date?

ANGIE: Mom told me what she's going to tell you. As I was headed out the door, she pulled me into the living room, gave me a very stern look and said, "Keep your hands folded and your legs crossed."

SYLVIA: That would've been good advice for Rodney and his fiancée.

ANGIE: Dad handles the boys differently, I suppose. I'm surprised they haven't come up here yet to harass you about this boy. Oh. *(pauses and leans in and studies Sylvia's face)* Uh-oh.

SYLVIA: What, uh-oh?

ANGIE: It looks like you've got a chaperone tonight.

SYLVIA darts over to the mirror.

SYLVIA: *(whines)* Noooooooo! This is so unfair.

ANGIE: I guess this first date is a little more stressful than you thought.

SYLVIA: What am I going to do? I can't pop it and there's no time to ice it or anything. Ugh! It's so red!

ANGIE: It's on your chin, so maybe you can wear a turtleneck?

SYLVIA: A turtleneck in May?

ANGIE: A scarf? Wrap it around your head like an old-time movie star. You'll be exotic and mysterious.

SYLVIA groans.

ANGIE: You could go in the opposite direction and wear something low-cut.

SYLVIA: *(whines)* This zit is larger than my boobs. I'm doomed.

SYLVIA flops on the bed and pouts.

SYLVIA: Well, at least I won't have to worry about a first kiss.

ANGIE: Pouting isn't going to help the situation. Besides, it's just a pimple. Everybody gets them. Charlie's probably had a few himself. *(gasps)* Maybe he's got pimples on his butt. Big, painful, still under the skin so they can't be popped pimples.

SYLVIA: Ugh, Angie! Gross! *(pulls her pillow over her face.)*

ANGIE: I'm only trying to make you feel better.

ANGIE moves over to SYLVIA'S bed to comfort her.

ANGIE: Look, he's going to be here in a few minutes and it's too late to cancel. If the zit really bothers you, I could go in your place.

SYLVIA: *(muffled under the pillow)* What?

ANGIE: Sure. You said you haven't spent much time with the guy and we look similar enough. I mean, you're certainly prettier than I am, but it'll be dark, especially in the movies. He'll never know the difference.

SYLVIA: *(still under the pillow)* I'm almost depressed enough to let you go.

ANGIE: Only almost? Then put on some make-up and find some shoes.

SYLVIA sighs as she tosses the pillow onto the bed, picks up her purse and returns to the mirror. She pulls a compact out and applies powder to her face.

SYLVIA: You should come with us.

ANGIE: And be your zit's date? That's a definite step up from Stanley, but not how I want to spend my Saturday night, thank you.

SYLVIA: C'mon! You want to meet Charlie and you shouldn't just sit at home.

ANGIE: Who will do the laundry?

SYLVIA: Pssh, Rodney should do it. He's gonna be a family man soon. It's time that he learned how to do that sort of stuff.

ANGIE: I don't know. This is your first date, just one of the many special events you'll remember for the rest of your life. You don't want it spoiled by your intimidating older sister tagging along.

SYLVIA finds a pair of shoes and slips them on.

SYLVIA: I don't want it spoiled by thuggish family members who might run off my date before we even get out of the house. Having some support by my side might not be so bad. You can watch my back and mock all the sleazy moves that boys make. We can sneak off to the bathroom and laugh about stuff.

ANGIE: And you're sure it wouldn't be awkward for you?

SYLVIA: I'm going on my very first date with a boy I hardly know, I can't wear my favourite shirt that everyone always compliments me on, and I have a tiny volcano on my face that could erupt at any moment. Tonight will be beyond awkward. If you're with me, maybe it won't be so embarrassing.

ANGIE: All right, you've convinced me. How long until he gets here? I need to find something to wear. I should've done the laundry earlier.

ANGIE picks through the laundry basket. SYLVIA looks at watch as a car horn honks.

ANGIE: *(shrugs)* Okay. You go downstairs and tell him he's got two dates tonight and I'll be right down.
SYLVIA: *(peeking out the window)* Hey, looks like I've got two dates, too!
ANGIE: What?
SYLVIA: He's got Molly's brother out in the car with him.
ANGIE: Which brother—the dorky junior high kid or the unbearably handsome college sophomore?
SYLVIA: It's the older one, Matt, who set up the date. I guess your cuteness meter isn't so rusty after all!
ANGIE: Yeah? Okay, let's get out of here before the brother brigade gets a whiff of the new blood.

SYLVIA pauses and looks at her sister.

SYLVIA: Thanks.
ANGIE: For letting you use my towel?
SYLVIA: For tonight, for being my sister.
ANGIE: You're welcome.

The girls share a short hug.

SYLVIA: C'mon! Let's get outta here!

The car horn honks again and the girls dash out of the room.

make
Love
Not
BABIES

TEASE OF THE SEABREEZE

(a stream of consciousness exercise inspired by the lists of words found in rounds of Boggle)

She was known as the Tease of the Seabreeze. The million-dollar mermaid of the community pool—elusive, graceful, alluring and bashful. Hers was an underwater ballet while others danced the aquatic watusi. Tens of teens gathered by the edge to glimpse the enchantress. Her presence made men tense and women ill at ease. From morning 'til dusk the bathing beauty remained immersed in the communal waters of questionable content. Loungers jokes about the ratio of water to chlorine to piss. Still, our miss could not be dissuaded. As tots waded and boys splashed, she glided through the liquid glass, oblivious.

Summer was over only when the water got too cold for her. Summer was over for good the day she left town. No one knew her name. No one knew her origins. Spectators speculated that she might turn pro. Whisper-prone rumor-mongers suggested the breaststroke Betty finally succumbed to princely pursuits and moved east. Summer months slipped away. Disappointed observers drifted to other destinations. Pool attendance nose dived with the main attraction's disappearance. No more splashes, no more kick boards, no more inner tubes.

The pool became a pit. A haven for families became a hangout for skaters and stoners. The Tease of the Seabreeze became simply a memory.

EVERY JOB
is a sales position

FELINE FRIENDLY

Who's that guy?
What's happening now?
Is the diver dude a villain?
Does this have subtitles?
NO! Don't go in the castle!
Is this Japanese?
Hey, Kev. You're over here a lot lately. You want to adopt Brian?
We're not ready to move in together! We're just hanging out.
See you tomorrow, Brian.
Hey, Kev. What's up?
We need to talk about Brian... UGH! I promised I wouldn't say anything, so please don't tell him I told you. Well, he's noticed that you've been distant and unaffectionate lately... He's not just a cat! He has feelings! He just wants what anyone else wants—to love and be loved... and he loves you, damnit!
...he loves you. I'm sorry, I have to go.
CALL KEVIN
RINGING..
MWROAWH

slantindicular

SOUND PROOF

It begins when the teacher sends home a note. I am mortified to be sent home with a teacher's note, knowing from televised situation comedies that teachers' notes are usually bad news, with the child in enough trouble to warrant a collective "oooh" from a studio audience. There had been a few real-life situations that could have been construed as wacky misunderstandings but were classified as questionable misconduct. Apparently, there were several instances where my response to a teacher's inquiry was inappropriate. I did not always take direction well. I was frequently answering to someone else's name. However, instead of asking me—a child probably lacking the moral compass to be truthful in a way that aligned with a pre-conceived truth—why on Earth I would behave in such ways, when most other evidence pointed to my being a quiet and clever child, the teacher sends me home with a note for my mother.

Several days later, my mother and I arrive at the state-funded Crippled Children's Clinic, where we sit amongst broken children and their tired parents until I am ushered away into a booth.

A soft-spoken lady with big hair and bigger shoulders, the latter likely built into her chunky-knit boldly-patterned sweater, guides me to the sole chair inside this small booth and secures large, heavy headphones around my petite ears. She checks that the headphones are properly plugged into the audio jack on a very sophisticated electronic panel with all sorts of shiny switches and buttons and those black-and-white embossed labels reading "DANGER" and "Do Not Touch." When she leans over to untangle the coiled headphone cords, I am nearly choked by the overwhelming scent of Elizabeth Taylor's White Diamonds perfume, which I recognize as my mother wore it for a few months until she decided she liked Elizabeth Taylor's Passion better. The scent hangs in the air long after the soft-spoken lady has done her best to prepare me for what to expect in here—explaining the process and demonstrating how to respond to the prompts through the headphones—and sequesters me in the booth, leaving only a vintage poster-sized diagram of the inner workings of the ear to keep me company.

I am familiar with the concept of this kind of booth as I've seen them in television game shows, where contestants are isolated from teammates to maintain an illusion of integrity in game play. This is not a game show. I will not be eligible to win fabulous prizes. I will not be sent home with a supply of turtle wax and Rice-a-Roni. This soundproof booth is an experiment, as we search for proof that sound is reaching me.

The booth has a window overlooking the rest of the lab. I can see the soft-spoken lady talking with an older, weathered woman with a severe pixie haircut, brown Gloria Vanderbilt glasses and a white lab coat. The soft-spoken lady is seated so I can only see the top of her teased bangs. The older woman looks over the soft-spoken lady's shoulder, occasionally gesturing at things around the computer desk on the other side of the booth.

The padded headphones form a hermetic seal around my ears, creating an uneasy and unnatural silence. I cannot hear myself exhale or cough or tap my fingers on the armrest. The nervous clacking of my teeth echoes in my skull. I figure if I sit here in silence long enough, I could almost convince myself that I can hear my own blinks. I gingerly bite my tongue to ease the chattering and I'm left alone with only my thoughts. I think about the meeting my mother had with the teacher to discuss my behaviour as outlined in the note. The teacher indicated that I might require special assistance. My mother inquired whether that I meant I should be placed in the special education

class. The teacher told my mother I was too clever, that special education was
for children who can't count to ten on their fingers and 12-year-olds who can't
get through *The Cat in the Hat* by themselves. They bandied about words like
"retarded" and "remedial" and determined that I was not. They agreed that
"handicapped" was a strong possibility.

The kids in my class do not look fondly on the special education class,
going so far as openly taunting them on the occasions we see them walking
to PE, hand-in-hand along the breezeway, as their honey-voiced teacher gently
encouraged them to stay together and walk carefully. The remedial group
was small, only eight or ten kids, with two teachers. At first, I thought these
kids were from the Remedial Age, time-traveling pals of King Arthur or
Robin Hood, simply misunderstood because they were of a different era.
I shared this theory with my mother one day and she set me straight about
the Middle Ages and the slim odds of Medieval time-travellers showing up
to attend a Southern elementary school in the 1980s. It was unlikely but it was
nicer to think of these kids as kind of strangers in a strange land than
as broken and inferior to the rest of us.

So deep into my own thoughts, I am startled when a woman's voice
crackles through the headphone speakers, telling me about tones and beeps
and how I should signal with my hand when I think I hear one. If I think
I hear a tone in my right ear, I should raise my right hand and similarly
with the left.

The tones roll in low, easing into my right ear. I raise my right hand.
A louder tone bounces to the left side. Up goes the left hand. Left again. Then
right. The tones get higher and faster and farther away. A few tones drift back
down, wafting into the auditory canal and quickly bouncing off the ear drum
back into the ether. I catch myself leaning forward, tilting my left ear,
as I think I hear a tone far off in the distance. But it is quiet. Perhaps it wasn't
a tone at all, just a memory of one lingering like the White Diamonds.

I sit in the eerie silence for a few minutes, presumably to cleanse the aural
palette of phantom tones still hovering mid-air. I look out the window of the
booth and no longer see the quiet lady's big hair. I wonder if the experiment
is over and whether someone will fetch me or maybe I have been forgotten.

How long would I have to sit alone in this booth before my mother, still waiting with the other stressed-out parents of abnormal children, would inquire about me and snatch me out of the room so that she could salvage what was left of the working day?

Eventually the woman crackles in the headphones to explain the next portion of the experiment. She explains that a recording will ask me to repeat the words I think I hear. I nod in reply. She explains again, asking then for verbal confirmation from me. I think I say "Okay."

The voice of God or maybe Thurl Ravenscroft thunders his commands through the headphone speakers "You will say the word—"

With misplaced confidence, the recorded man guides me through a series of common one- and two-syllable words. Amidst the clicks and buzzes of a cassette tape that has been unspooled and respooled hundred of times, I must instantly determine whether I will say the word "weigh" or one of its three dozen homophones and rhymes. In the four seconds between the recorded prompts, I pit logic and reason against instinct and reflex. The English language—so rich, so complex, so extremely frustrating in these moments. In reading, one would hardly confuse goats with coasts and coats with gauche. Would Tony the Tiger expect a seven-year-old to even know the word "gauche"? None of the other seven-year-olds in my class knew it, when the teacher read my spelling test aloud to the class last week. "Use this word in a sentence," was the teacher's instruction. I took a guess at which word she said, and was wrong. However, all the words I did use were spelled correctly, so I got partial credit for "The gauche ghost wore a coat on the coast, quotes the goat." Stuff that in your hat, Mr. Cat.

I say the words "jewel" and "woods" and "potion" and "clock" and "boy" and "witch" and "bottle." If this were a fairytale MadLib, I'd say there's trouble brewing in a forest. I am given no indication whether I have repeated Thurl's words verbatim. No perceptible ding or buzz, no "You should have said 'school' or 'which' or 'ocean' or 'throttle,'" which makes for an entirely different story.

The commands stop abruptly, along with the ambient hisses and whirrs of the cassette. The big-haired lady comes in to release me from the booth, carefully removing the headphones and directing me to a chair at a table near the control panel outside of the booth. I am immediately comforted by the normal dull hums of overhead lighting and electronic cooling fans and the sight of my mother, who was brought in for the results of the experiment.

I haven't the opportunity to share with my mother my experience with floating tones or my idea for a new fairytale before we're joined by the older, harsh-looking woman I saw from the booth. The woman is revealed to be an audiologist who, despite first impressions, is kind and animated and engaging when talking my perpetually worried mother through my freshly diagnosed condition. We are shown graphs and charts while the audiologist says the words "moderate" and "severe" and "frequency" and "decibel" and "sibilant" and "fricatives." We are given pamphlets and highlighted photocopies from textbooks describing "sensorineural hearing loss" and what can be done about it. I am taken to another room where blue putty is smushed into my ears. As swiftly as I was whisked away, the blue putty is removed and I am returned to my mother with instructions to come back to the clinic a few weeks later.

In school, I have transformed from Problem Child to a Special Needs Child. The teacher, once exasperated with my quirky habit of answering "here" for Jasmine Hiller, showers me with special treatment by moving me to the front row and taking particular care in speaking loudly and slowly to me in a way that makes me wish I could just take home a note to my mother every day. I've also been awarded thrice-weekly sessions one-on-one with a speech therapist, who will fetch me from my regular classwork to spend 45 minutes in the kickball storage trailer teaching me things like how to say the words "speech therapist" and "thrice."

Back at the state-funded Crippled Children's Clinic, I am outfitted with a refurbished pair of beige-yet-still-conspicuous hearing aids for a trial run. The audiologist tells me they are programmed to pick up certain frequencies. I am disappointed when she clarifies that I will not receive Casey Kasem's weekly Top 40 directly into my auditory canal. One boy in my class will be similarly disappointed when he learns that I am not in direct contact with aliens, who are transmitting test answers to my devices for nefarious space purposes that require a second grader to pass a quiz about Charlotte's Web.

When the audiologist powers up the hearing aids, suddenly the whole world is audibly illuminated. I am paralyzed and excited by the distorted cacophony of sounds, eager to distinguish and catalog all these new noises —dogs chirping, children barking, bird wings flapping, tree branches wrestling in the wind, other people chewing, distant train whistles crying, faint rappings upon chamber doors. I can almost believe that I hear paint drying and grass growing.

As days go by, I notice that everything is louder—ringing telephones, squeaking chairs, clattering utensils in the chatter-filled cafetorium, fingernails scratching against skin—I don't know how normal people live with all this. It's like being given a 64-pack of crayons after a lifetime of colouring with an eight-pack. How does one take on the seemingly insurmountable challenge of filtering out the unnecessary and inoculating one's mind against things like the high-pitched hums of appliances?

How can anyone hear themselves think in all this racket?!

Yes, everything is definitely much louder but not necessarily clearer.

Voices are distorted.

Noises are uniformly amplified, so I can't tell which direction they're coming from.

The kids in my class are perturbed about all the preferential treatment I'm getting and make sure their grievances well heard, even without hearing aids. The car radio is a source of early morning irritation as my mother listens to the traffic report while driving me to school. I find my speech therapist, a former audiologist, to be the sole sympathizer to my predicament.

She shows me a diagram of the word CAT with huge chunks removed from it so it only looks like:

(/ |

She explains to me that in my particular condition, there are sounds that I will never hear. The damage has been done. There will always be pieces of words missing and I will always have to work harder to fill in the gaps. My ability to hear those pieces is gone forever. Even with the most advanced piece of technology providing sophisticated amplification—just like writing these symbols larger—

$$(\quad / \quad |$$

Making those sounds louder won't amplify the pieces I need to make CAT. Or his hat, I presume.

After a few weeks, I start to long for the isolation booth with its artificial silence. I spend less time wearing the devices. My speech therapist offers a few handy survival techniques for living without the devices. She shows me how to sit like a mafioso—angled in my desk with my back to the wall, positioned so entrances and people are easily visible and no one can sneak up behind me—to minimize confusion and misunderstandings. She teaches me about the sounds I'll never really hear, like "hw" in "which" and "whether" and "whip." She explains it all to my mother, who is relieved to find we don't have to keep the hearing aids and she no longer needs to fret over these expensive devices getting lost or stolen.

We return the beige contraptions to the clinic so they can be refurbished again for the next child who gets sent home with a teacher's note. I settle into a life of quiet frustration—never quite certain of sounds, never quite getting the gist of group conversations, always careful not to frustrate others by asking "what?" and "hunh?" and "could you repeat that?" and "okay, could you rephrase that in a slightly different way using fewer words that sound like other very common words?" Always calculating whether it's worth the hassle of explaining my condition to strangers. Are we in a Very Special Episode, where we use my hearing loss is a teachable moment, or are we in a farce, where my misunderstanding of a simple inquiry sets off a chain of embarrassing yet hilarious events? I am sad that I will never hear a spider weaving her web or bees laughing or the triangles and tambourines in my favourite songs or my mobile telephone ringing at the bottom of my purse. I am always thinking about the phantom tones drifting through the air just out of reach.

You are
only as good
as the last
sandwich
you ate.

WE'RE TOAST

Every day is the same.
The human staggers into the kitchen and flips on the overhead light.
She opens the fridge and retrieves the orange juice and grape jelly.
She groggily fumbles for the bread bag, where I and my brethren reside.
The crusty guard is shoved aside as my brothers cower, whimpering
and praying not to be chosen.
She grabs two of my family members and locks the rest of us back
 in our cellophane cell.
I watch through the tinted plastic as the human tosses my brothers
into their own personal hell.
I hear their screams through the orange glow radiating from the toaster.
The rest of us cower in fear, wishing that we could escape and be free.
We envy the carefree stalks of wheat not yet subjected to this torment.
Soon, my brothers emerge from the hellscape. They are darker and wiser.
They have seen the afterlife and only survive a few moments longer
to tell the tale before being devoured by the cruel human.
It is our destiny to be consumed.
We serve our purpose.
Some of us are spared the heat, employed to envelop cold meats and cheeses.
Others are ripped apart and tossed onto the ground, to be pecked away
by street fowl.
Tomorrow I shall be moldy and miss my chance at being devoured.
Tomorrow will be a blessed day.

THE MEME ACCORDING TO CARK

There once was a fella called Marc
who was jonesin' for a caffeine spark
When he ordered his coffee
he said "Marc with a C"
But the barista made a latte for Cark

That's certainly the legend spreading across the vast Internet superhighway, anyway. My name is Cark and I am Internet famous. Or, rather, my name is Internet famous. One year ago, on an ordinary Tuesday, I ordered my regular fancy coffee drink from a popular fancy coffee chain, like I do on ordinary Tuesdays. I recall this particular Tuesday because I made a special trip to renew my gold status in the rewards program, which was set to expire that week. In the months prior, I'd shifted my loyalties to the independent coffee place in my office building. But I still like to treat myself during birthday week to a free frothy mocha drink, courtesy of the rewards program. So I went in, queued up, placed my order for my grande, half-caf soy cinnamon latte with caramel drizzle, picked it up at the end of the counter, then continued with the rest of my boring little day. Three days later, my sister sent me a link to a photo posted on snapchat that was going viral. It was my cup with my name and the code for my complex concoction with the caption "i said my name was marc with a c."

Suddenly, it was everywhere. My cup was being shared by strangers on Reddit, Tumblr, Facebook, Flickr, Instagram, Pinterest, and even the long neglected LiveJournal. Every man called Marc is now being forwarded a photo of my Starbucks cup with the caption "I said my name was Marc with a C." People comment to complain about baristas forever bungling simple names. There are Tumblrs dedicated to sharing cups with mangled monikers. It was through one of these blogs that I happened to see the "I said my name was Stephen with a PH" meme featuring a receipt spelling the name "Phteven." Phteven predates my meme by several months. It seems that some social media expert must have deduced that Cark is catchier, zippier than Phteven, and has better traction for virality several times over.

I am no stranger to being misidentified. Throughout grade school, my teachers called me Clark. My first girlfriend called me Carl for three months. My supervisor's boss insists that my name is Kirk. My own Starbucks cup has come up as Carla on several occasions. This meme, however, is a first.

Cark is an old family name. When the last of the Carks perished, new generations elected to honour the memory by bestowing the former surname onto newer generations. The rest of the men in my family leave the name safely buried in the middle, reducing it to an initial and going about their life Cark-free. My parents were saddled with the chore of paying homage to two great dead men, which is how I came to be known as Evelyn Cark Schmutzfänger. I've pleaded with my mother to let me change one of my names but family tradition was more important than the relentless torment of her precious child. For a few glorious years—thanks to high metabolism and a pallor befitting a guy with a proclivity for staying indoors with television and video games—I was given the slightly cooler nickname Carcass.

Now I'm just plain old Cark. Or, I was until Carkbucks happened and every guy called Marc who's ever had to say "It's Marc with a 'C'" suddenly gets this Cark cup meme from people they haven't heard from in years—school friends, distant relatives, the ex-girlfriends of guys Marc doesn't even hang out with anymore. I know what the Marcs are going through because some of them have tracked down my email and complained, at length, about how they're getting this "joke" sent to them. A couple of them have sent nasty messages telling me to stop mocking them, to stop encouraging the meme. They believe that my name on my social media profile is taking the "joke" too far.

On my Instagram, I posted a photo of my most recent Starbucks cup with my name hastily scribbled on the side and my cherished gold card, with my name clearly printed on the front. Cark Schmutzfänger — member since 2013, long before this stupid meme. People just laugh, tack it onto the original Snapchat image and claim Sbux just gets it wrong everywhere.

Is it fair to blame the employees of an international coffee chain? Sure, baristas are notorious for getting names wrong, but who wouldn't, with the din and buzz and whirring blenders at the height of the morning rush. Coffee cups aren't the only way our names get screwed up. In general everyday conversation, people are constantly misunderstanding each other and using their internal—frequently faulty—auto-fill and auto-correct functions. They only listen to the first part of a name, question, or answer to a basic inquiry, and fill in the rest automatically under the assumption that they know what you mean. Sometimes they believe they misheard you—or you misspoke—and adjust what they heard to what they believe you meant. Hilarity ensues. Embarrassment abounds. Cark becomes Clark and Carl and Kirk and Carol and Cartman and Corky and Cook and Mark. And when you try to correct them, they'll make excuses like, "Well, you look like a Carl" or "I guess I'm thinking of someone else this guy's introduced me to." The coffee industry isn't a threat to personal brands—it's the whole human race.

I changed my name on Facebook for a while, at the height of Carkbucks. When I shared a link to a news story about how there's so much garbage in the ocean, we pretty much definitely have plastic in our diet, an aunt posted a comment underneath that said "Yikes. Hey, why did you change your name? I didn't recognize you and almost unfriended you." This from the woman who, for my last birthday commented "HBD Cerk." What hope can we have for humanity when our Facebook friends can't get the spelling of our names correct while wishing us happy birthdays when the name right there next to the box they just typed "hbd" into?

                                    slantindicular

Look, it was my cup. It was presumptuous of that Marc guy to lay claim to it. Now Marcs the world over are getting Cark cups and I'm getting harassed because a lot of people have a banal sense of humour. I can't even order fancy coffee drinks with my own name anymore because the baristas are hip to the meme now. When I give my name, the kid scribbling on my cup gives me a knowing smirk, like I'm trying to trick him. I can't go to other cafes with pick-up counters where they shout your name for fear of a Marc encounter. My gold reward membership status is in serious danger. The worst part is that neither I nor the originator of the meme can parlay this Internet fame into monetary gains. Hashtag: first world problem.

Eventually the meme will be forgotten by the masses. Aunts and acquaintances will pass along another viral LOL they picked up from their cousins and church buddies. They won't understand the lingering resentment, irritation, fear, and pain caused by their clueless Carkening. My friends will go back to ridiculing my top knot and my keytar instead of saying, "Hey, did you see that meme? That's hiLARious!" But I'll never again be able to meet a Marc without apologizing for my own name.

At least I know my name isn't Phteven.

GRANDPA GIRLFRIEND

A couple discusses a development that could impact their relationship.

GIRLFRIEND - early 30s, wearing bulky cardigan with pockets and big glasses on chain around neck, wardrobe and mannerisms that would befit an elderly man
BOYFRIEND - early 30s, youthful casual dress, contrast from girlfriend's attire

BOYFRIEND enters and joins his GIRLFRIEND at café table.

BOYFRIEND: Sorry I'm late, I just got your text. What's wrong?
GIRLFRIEND: Oh, nothing's wrong.
BOYFRIEND: But you have something important to tell me?
GIRLFRIEND: Yes. (*pauses, unsure how to break the news, then announces excitedly*) I'm a Grandpa!
BOYFRIEND: Hey! —Bu...what?
GIRLFRIEND: I'm a Grandpa.
BOYFRIEND: I don't know what that means. Do you have some family that I don't know about?

GIRLFRIEND: *(scoffs)* No.

BOYFRIEND: Well, uh, did you adopt someone who has kids?

GIRLFRIEND: Of course not.

BOYFRIEND: I guess I don't understand.

GIRLFRIEND: As you know, I recently had a big birthday and that got me asking myself a lot of questions. Who am I? What am I doing with my life? What do I see for my future? I have done a lot of soul searching, trying to determine my place in the world, in society, and I've finally found it.

BOYFRIEND: *(still trying to process the concept)* Wait...a grandfather?

GIRLFRIEND: Grandpa.

BOYFRIEND: So...you want to be a grandfather? How's that gonna work? How will that affect us? Are you transitioning? Oh god! I don't know what to say without sounding insensitive. What can I say? Am I allowed to ask questions? I have so many questions!

GIRLFRIEND: Calm down. Obviously I'm not a literal grandfather. I'm simply self-identifying as a Grandpa because that's the lifestyle that most comfortably defines me.

BOYFRIEND: Why not be a grandmother? You could take up knitting? Or baking!

GIRLFRIEND: Ugh, knitting. I need a new hobby at my age? Grandmothers are expected to be warm and compassionate and cuddly. Grandpas have no responsibilities. They don't have to tolerate children. They don't have to tolerate anything! They can be racist and make insensitive, off-colour remarks and people think it's adorable. They can dress comfortably. They can tell terrible jokes—I love terrible jokes! As a grandpa, I can play chess in the park in the middle of the afternoon. I can watch the old dubya-dubya two pictures on television.

BOYFRIEND: Well, you are kind of racist and you do love movies about Nazis.

GIRLFRIEND: I don't love the Nazis. I love pictures about beating the Nazis.

BOYFRIEND: Still, a lady grandfather? That's not how nature works. Don't you think it's a bit...privileged of you to self-identify in a masculine way. If you weren't a white woman, you wouldn't be able to pull this off.

GIRLFRIEND: How dare you! I'm blazing a trail for people of all kinds to be able to live openly as Grandpas.

BOYFRIEND: This is too weird.

GIRLFRIEND: If you can't handle this, I got a full bag of Werther's Originals and the boxset of Matlock at home, so... *(starts to leave)*

BOYFRIEND: No, it's not you. Well, it's you a little bit. I mean, I think it's great that you've found yourself. It's just...this is not the first time a woman has had a personal identity awakening with me.

GIRLFRIEND: Oh yeah?

BOYFRIEND: Something about dating me triggers an epiphany about a woman's sense of self, I guess? My first girlfriend turned into a Mermaid. My girlfriend at university determined she was a Juggalo. One woman realized she was a Brony. Another became a nudist...that wasn't so bad except she was a sushi chef. One girlfriend left me for one of her characters in The Sims game and married him last year...they just adopted Tamagotchi triplets. And my last girlfriend self-identified as a sloth—the animal not the sin.

GIRLFRIEND: They all sound adorable.

BOYFRIEND: What happened to normal women?!

GIRLFRIEND: That's not a thing.

BOYFRIEND: *(shrill)* Lady Grandpa isn't a thing!

GIRLFRIEND: Lemme tell you something—this culture is so obsessed with youth. Forty is the new twenty, sixty is the new middle-aged, and thirty-five is barely legal. 'Adult' means something dirty and 'Mature' means you're over the hill. No one wants to be old and yet our bodies continue to age. I'm watching the Generation X get gray and wrinkly and frail. My disaffected heroes are now afflicted with aches and pains, thinking about life insurance and walk-in tubs. The whole aging population gets lumped together under the zippy label 'Zoomer' because no one can really retire and active 70-year-olds bristle at being called elderly. Where do I fit in? I'm gonna grow old before I'm allowed to grow up. I've gotta go buy my pants at Forever 21 to play along with society's charade and maintaining a facade of youth. I didn't like being a teenager the first time, why should I fight to hold onto a part of life that I don't identify with simply because society romanticizes it? Human bodies naturally deteriorate and yet people would rather inject themselves full of suspect chemicals so that someone still finds them sexually desirable—which is based on an antiquated biological need to reproduce. In my day, old people were allowed to be old. They weren't relevant anymore, but they could sit down and wear loose-fitting pants and soak their teeth in peace. Look, I don't mean to fetishize the elderly. The inevitable deterioration of the human body is terrible and I'm in no rush to experience that. I just feel that the 'grandpa' as a subculture has a lot more sartorial freedom and fewer societal expectations. By the time I am legitimately elderly, we'll be going to rave parties in the all-purpose room in the nursing home and watching Brett and Blaine pop wheelies on their Rascals. " Oh! Look how vibrant and active we all are! Age is just a number! Ignore the cracking of my crumbling bones—that just means I'm still alive!" Why does the grocery store sound like a night club?! We didn't start the fire but maybe we should consider putting it out soon because the smoke is clouding sensible thinking. Youth may well be wasted on the young but comfort is wasted on the old. I just want to wear my cardigans, watch my classic movies, and yell at a few clouds while I can enjoy it.

The couple sit in silence for a moment.

BOYFRIEND: Yep. you're a Grandpa, alright.
GIRLFRIEND: So? Where does that leave us?
BOYFRIEND: Well, nothing's really changed, right?
GIRLFRIEND: Still me. Just a more comfortable me.
BOYFRIEND: I do want you to be comfortable. You know I've never really gone for the heavy eye make-up and the stilettos and the hair products. It all looks like an awful lot of work.
GIRLFRIEND: This is what I'm saying.
BOYFRIEND: And nothing else would change? You're not gonna make me call you by some old-man name like Morty or Elmer?
GIRLFRIEND: Someday you'll be an old man, *Kyle*.

BOYFRIEND: Fair point.

GIRLFRIEND: *(pulls a hard candy out of the pocket of her cardigan and seductively unwraps it)* You, uh, wanna go back to my place and I'll read *The Princess Bride* to you again?

BOYFRIEND: Will there be kissing?

GIRLFRIEND: It's not inconceivable.

BOYFRIEND: As you wish.

GIRLFRIEND wordlessly offers the unwrapped candy to BOYFRIEND.
He nods. She feeds him the candy and they smile contentedly.

CHRONIC CREATIVITY

I need to talk about something very serious. It's about a condition that
I have been living with for many years. Nobody seems to know much about it
or how to cure it. You see, I suffer from chronic creativity.

As a child, I was constantly inventing worlds and imagining situations.
My toy box was a spaceship. My tape recorder was a radio station. My light
switch was a drive-thru intercom. I wrote songs and plays and stories. My toys
were cast in fibrefill vaudeville and Barbie burlesques.

My mother could sense something different about me. The way I put my
puzzles together upside down. The way I said "updown side" instead of upside
down. The way I organized my crayons by personality traits instead of colour.
She tried her best to protect me from the outside world (or was is outworld
side?) and vice versa. We tried to harness and suppress my creative urges.
We tried to channel them into socially acceptable and productive projects.
We did all the creative tests. I went through creative therapy. I tried the
creative aids. Nothing worked.

I was ridiculed in school for my inappropriate outbursts of creativity,
but I just couldn't control it. As you can imagine (DON'T! That's how it starts!),
creativity made it impossible to function in "normal" society. The Urges come on

suddenly and without warning. In one minute I'm thinking about sandwiches and the next I'm furiously scribbling on nearby scraps of paper or flesh.

Sadly, being creative does not necessarily signify great skill or talent. Like how being chatty doesn't mean one is also eloquent and well-versed. Quality of output varies. Opinions of quality of output wildly varies. The production of ideas often outpaces the ability the process and capture ideas. These ideas can get lost and mangled. Chronic creativity is an unpredictable condition. No one knows when a flare up will occur; we can only hope to manage the attacks. I can go several weeks without incident. I once went five years without a single creative impulse.

Is it chemical imbalance? Is it contagious?

Is it genetic? Is it genius? Is it a blocked nostril?

I don't know. But it's a very serious and very real condition.

Treatment and management of creativity is costly and time-consuming and often requires special equipment. The trouble is that I'm interested in a variety of creative pursuits and I often fall prey to the notion of "Hell, I could do that." Alas, hell, I could not do that. Or that. Or that, either, though I will convince myself I was kind of okay at that. I am not naturally brilliant at anything so far. Some creatives can switch gears between multiple disciplines elegantly and brilliantly. When I switch gears there's grinding and scraping sounds and a bunch of unhappy people backed up behind me.

Creativity is a lot of work. Let's say I've written a book. It isn't enough to write a book, one must devise creative ways to promote the book—start a blog, host a podcast, make a viral video, design a website, write clever tweets, take Insta-worthy photos…The thought of all the work is almost enough to extinguish the creative flame. Almost.

Right now I sit in a pile of my own mediocrity. Things made out of perceived necessity. Skills developed half-assedly and cobbled together from poorly written online tutorials. Great ideas destroyed by poor execution. I know just enough to be dangerous but not enough to be successful.

I'm a creative hyphenate. I'm a dabbler.

I am a vessel. I am a tool.

I wear a lot of hats.

But maybe I shouldn't. Maybe I should focus on one creative outlet, plug in and concentrate my energy on mastering a single skill. Can I commit to one creative outlet? Do I need a special adapter?

If you know someone who is afflicted with this condition, try to be patient with them. Be kind about their creative output. Keep them well stocked in pens and paper. Give them gift cards to coffee shops and grocery stores. Hire them to create materials for your business or event. Pay them for said materials. Click "Like" on their silly projects on Facebook. Organize a marathon to raise money for creativity research.

My great hope is to one day be cured of this ailment. I'd like to merely exist for a while, with no compulsive need to frantically scribble some half-baked whimsies. In the meantime, do you need a scarf?
I'm learning how to knit.

"Can you validate my existence?"

Some People Just Can't Say No (I Can't Say Anything Else)

When someone makes you a resistible offer
There's one answer that you can proffer

Use a two-letter word that's so taboo
If I can say it, so can you

When I receive an invitation
for a night out on the town
I am of the inclination
to turn that invite down

In response to your RVSP,
you don't need to guess
I won't need a party dress
when I don't circle yes

If you're prone
to give the cold shoulder
Throw 'em a bone, be a bit bolder

Forget the brush off,
don't simply rush off

Why keep 'em in suspense
and make a situation tense

Give it go,
deliver the blow
and just say —

Vo-dee-oh-dee-oh—
Vo-dee-oh-dee-oh—
Vo-dee-oh-dee-
oh-NO!

THE ART OF SITTING QUIETLY

Are you tired of always being the centre of attention? Does it usually fall to you to keep conversations lively at parties? Are you naturally loquacious and prone to talking to anyone in your general proximity? Are you frequently regaling fellow queue-joiners with your favourite queue anecdotes? Do you incessantly initiate chit-chat with strangers in waiting rooms? Do you find yourself compulsively ejaculating comments into nearby discussions? Is your social circle shrinking because friends are intimidated by your bombastic personality? Are you actually relieved when you're not invited to things because you didn't really want to tell the story about making eye contact with Richard Kind from a bus stop for the gazillionth time? Don't you wish someone else could dominate the conversation for a while? Aren't you curious to hear a voice other than your own?

Maybe it's time you learned how to sit quietly!

Enroll now in The Art of Sitting Quietly in Places virtual correspondence course and start learning how you can successfully sit quietly in public places. With this instructional 87-part series, you'll be able to sit quietly on a bus, at a party, and in a café. You can even sit quietly while at home or at work!

Attending an event without chairs? No problem! The Art of Sitting Quietly in Places will even show you how to stand unobtrusively!

Register for The Art of Sitting Quietly in Places and acquire the skills you need to manage your response to common conversational triggers such as "Hello" and "Some weather, huh?" and "Are you waiting for the washroom?" Sign up now and you'll gain exclusive access to The Art of Sitting Quietly in Places webinar, where you'll learn how to resist engaging with others by staring out of windows, napping with your eyes open, looking down the street for your friend who should be arriving shortly, and pretending to be interested in historic plaques on the sides of buildings.

Subscribe to The Art of Sitting Quietly in Places free lifestyle newsletter and each week you'll receive lessons on the different types of sitting quietly, such as attentive listening, quiet reflection, silent judging, and wistful rumination.

Once you've mastered your sitting quietly technique, you'll be ready to advance to nodding politely and murmuring appreciatively. The Art of Sitting Quietly in Places bonus video podcast will show you how to still seem engaged while surreptitiously texting, contemplating your own navel, or daydreaming about sandwiches. You'll learn eight completely natural-sounding interjections and responses to disguise when you've been tuning out conversations. Impress acquaintances and co-workers with your new reserved persona by demonstrating a "sincere interest" in their small talk. With the help of The Art of Sitting Quietly in Places, you'll be a sparkling non-versationalist in no time!

Still not sure if sitting quietly is right for you? Studies show that people who sit quietly live longer, more productive lives and are generally considered more intelligent and sexually desirable than those who blabber constantly. People who have completed The Art of Sitting Quietly in Places program noticed an increase in party invitations, clearer complexion, faster queues, and a reciprocal silent nod of acknowledgement from Richard Kind in a crowded coffee shop.

Ready to embrace your inner introvert through The Art of Sitting Quietly in Places? Then sit down and shut up right now!

WORD LORD

(a stream of consciousness exercise inspired by the lists of words found in rounds of Boggle)

some work with wood, others with wool
his tools are adverbs, adjectives and nouns
his stories told to tots in their beds
his wit is a hit with twits young and old
his quotables quoted, his notables noted
the word lord spins yarns of metaphors and the metaphysical
tongue-twisted tales of two-toed toads tied to tooting tit-willows
tow-headed tots tooted their loot—a rod, a kite, and a flute
who could forget when the bee lost a bet with a beet?
the word lord advises the inadvisable
woes will wane with the rain
don't hide from the tide, take root in the sand and let life wash over you, calmly
scholars try to make sense of his nonsense, dig deep for depth, searching for
soul in the soulless
critics don't miss a beat
some words will erode, fade from collective consciousness
new wordsmiths will trot out their modern wit
the word lord's reign is short-lived but long recalled

STOP EXPECTING
THE WORST
WHEN YOU CAN
BE THE WORST!

the future is probably
disappointed in us

ABOUT KATHARINE!

Katharine is the author of *The Curable Romantic: Advice for the Romance-Impaired*, the best-selling *30 Failures by Age 30, Slantindicular: Stories Among Other Things* and the author-illustrator of *BORIS: Robot of Leisure.*
Katharine also an artist and graphic designer specializing in low-brow pop art inspired by 20th century popular culture. Katharine's paintings, part of her Robot of Leisure series, have been exhibited in galleries and public spaces across North America.
View more of her work at thatkatharine.com.